BOOK 1 OF THE
MANIFEST DESTINY SERIES

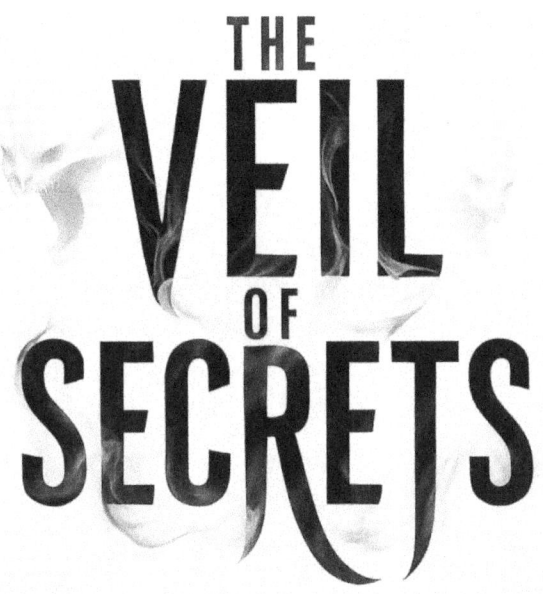

THE VEIL OF SECRETS

BETSEY KULAKOWSKI

AND JB CAINE

BUSY QUILL PRESS

CONTENTS

DEDICATION

For the ones we lost — and the ones who brought us back.

— B.K. & J.B.C.

MORE FROM BETSEY KULAKOWSKI AND JB CAINE

Join the adventure with Betsey and the VERITAS CODEX series!

www.authorbetseykulakowski.com

SCAN ME

Keep the magic alive with JB Caine and the Arcana Trilogy, the Ironshield's Shadow Series, and YOUR STORY Adventures!

www.jbcaine.com

SCAN ME

PROLOGUE

IN THE BEGINNING

London, April 6, 1682 – St. Paul's Cathedral

The night air tasted of soot and salt as Sir Christopher Wren descended into the unfinished crypt beneath the rising dome of St. Paul's Cathedral. A single lantern swung overhead, casting distorted shadows across scrolls of blueprints scattered about on the work table.

Stone walls, newly chiseled, bore notations in chalk — but older marks remained faintly visible beneath. Weathered symbols had been etched by unknown hands long before the cathedral rose: a Sumerian cuneiform seal half-erased by time, a faint Eye of Horus beside a star-chart traced in ochre, and near the eastern arch, a geometric motif common to early Islamic mysticism, its lines whispering of constellations and forgotten alignments.

The Manifest sat on the pedestal nearby. He moved the candle to illuminate the exposed page of the ancient tome. A chill passed through him, as much from the cold of the stone chamber as from the ancient mysteries held within. The pages came alive with shifting ink, not just names and objects, but the intentions behind the objects' creation. Every cursed artifact, lost relic, or sealed horror the Aegis Order had secured was recorded within. Things meant to be forgotten were remembered within the pages.

With a shivering hand, he closed the cover and inscribed a final cipher along the outer edge of the binding, using a drop of his own blood as ink. The sacrificial key tied into the harmonic frequencies and starlight geometry. It was his sacred charge to protect all the relics, the Manifest included. This would be his greatest duty to the Order.

*Do you truly believe **you** are worthy?* the book whispered to him.

From the shadows, low voices rose in unison. "You bind what should be free." Seven robed men stepped from the shadowed corridor, led by a woman cloaked in sable and silver. "You think architecture can keep the truth from blooming? You hide the seeds of knowledge from the sun, but you merely delay their emergence into the light, Wren."

Christopher anticipated this day would come. The Obsidian Covenant had been on his heels for years. He moved closer to the Manifest, sensing the pulsing desire to be taken by anyone powerful enough to wield it. But Wren knew what it was capable of, and the secrets hidden within. He had witnessed what it did to the last Keeper who tried to read it cover to cover.

"There is nothing here for you but your own destruction." Wren placed his body between his rival and the book.

"I hear the Manifest's call, just as you do," she said.

"No man nor woman may claim to be its master," Wren said, twisting the candelabra into the pedestal with a mechanical grind. The floor trembled, and the scrolls on the table began to roll toward the edge. Books on the shelves shivered, drawing inward while the stone walls groaned and began to rotate. A series of mechanical clicks echoed throughout the chamber. Chests in niches on the walls, filled with ancient relics, locked themselves tight without keys. Inner walls began to rise into the ceiling above, leaving blank stone behind. Dust billowed from the ancient tiles, curling upward with each groan of the shifting structure. The chamber had awakened to guard what it held.

"Seize what you can!" the woman commanded her troops, lunging for the pedestal. As her hand contacted the leather bound tome, a scream erupted through the shifting chamber, an explosion of light illuminating the room with a brilliance so dazzling that the dark soldiers recoiled.

Wren locked eyes with his mortal foe, challenging her, knowing what the Manifest was capable of. "You have no right to bind its power," she hissed.

"The Manifest will decide for itself who may read its pages," he answered, as the chamber door lowered. It would seal them in, and there would be no escape ... as far as she knew.

The bells of St. Paul's Cathedral began a dissonant clanging ... sound from a bell tower that had not yet been completed. She reached for the book, and her hand passed through nothingness, the Manifest having spirited itself to safety. "What is the meaning of this?"

"The Manifest has chosen its master," he smirked. "And it was not you."

"This isn't over," she snarled, and then turned to her men. "We're out of time!" She grabbed a scroll in one hand and made a run for the exit. The foot soldiers of the Obsidian Covenant made a desperate grab for what relics they could, and, following the lead of their Mistress, scurried out the door before the concrete block could trap them within.

1

A Study in Charcoal and Blood

Present Day

Niall Roth stumbled out of the Sevenoaks Station and ducked into a shop doorway to make sure he hadn't been followed. There was a chill in the November air, and he was grateful for it. The early dusk and bustling crowds gave him cover. He watched the London Road exit for a couple of minutes, and once satisfied, he crossed over to Hitchen Hatch Lane and tried to look inconspicuous despite the bloody lip and emerging bruise along his left cheek. The other injuries were hidden by his coat, and he pulled it tight around him.

If he could just get to Wrens' place, he could claim Sanctuary. Even with the semi-bad blood between them, Beatrice couldn't deny him shelter, and he could nurse his injuries and get his prize into safer hands.

An elderly couple walking a froufrou white dog (complete with a Union Jack bow between its ears) gave him a sideways glance as he passed them on the sidewalk, and he was fairly certain he heard the woman mutter the word *pub* as soon as they thought they were out of earshot. He smirked, glad that they'd supplied their own explanation for his appearance and wishing that he'd gotten his arse kicked over a pint rather than at the hands of the Covenant's thugs.

Beatrice's house came into view, and there were lights on in the sitting room. He imagined her sitting by the fireplace reading one of her dusty old books. The thought warmed him, but the feeling passed quickly when he considered that her husband Simon might well add another bruise to his face if he was the one to open the door.

Niall hazarded another glance behind him, and seeing no one, he made his way across the cobbled drive. He ducked behind the safety of a hedge that partially obscured the door. Then he rang the bell and waited, nervous at the reception he might get. His mission's success would override any personal vendettas, he decided, so when he heard footsteps approaching, he let his shoulders relax. The latch clicked and the door swung inward.

"Sanctu ..." he began, but stopped when he saw the young woman studying him from the doorway.

"Can I help you? If you're peddling anything, we aren't interested." Her sandy blond hair was draped over her shoulder in a messy braid, and she crossed her arms over her chest as he fumbled for a response. She was the perfect picture of Beatrice in her younger days, but with an edge to her that Beatrice had never had, at least not while he'd known her. One of her daughters, then, certainly.

"I ... I'm looking for Beatrice and Simon Wren," he stammered.

"They're on holiday in Spain. You'd know that if you'd phoned first. What's this about?" She narrowed her eyes at him, panic sinking in as his escape plan began to crumble.

"I ... uh, I'm a friend of theirs from ... work, and ..." One would think he'd be better at making up cover stories by now.

There was a spark of recognition in the woman's eyes and then a glare. "What were you saying when I opened the door?"

He hesitated a moment, but her possible knowledge of the Order was his only chance. "S-sanctuary."

"Come inside, then, quickly." She ushered him in and locked the door. His breath whooshed out in relief as he stood in the foyer. "This is highly irregular," she chided him. "But I'll help if I can. Who are you?" She indicated for him to sit on a leather loveseat in the tiny study just inside the door.

"I'm Niall Roth. I've been on a mission." He couldn't think of anything else to add since he wasn't sure how much Simon and Beatrice had told their children. Three of them, he remembered now. It had been so long.

"My name's Eliza," the woman said. "Stay here and I'll get some ice for your face." She turned abruptly and headed down the hallway toward the kitchen. "ESME!" she yelled up the stairs. "Esme, get down here!"

In the kitchen, Eliza fumbled with the plastic bag's seal, silently cursing the fact that these *convenient zipper seals* were rarely convenient at all. After a moment's struggle, she managed to pull the sides apart so she could fill the bag with ice. She grabbed a clean tea towel from the drawer, making sure it wasn't one of the monogrammed ones, just in case she couldn't get the blood stains out later.

Esme hadn't emerged, of course. No doubt she was painting something and was far away in her imagination, unaware that Eliza had even summoned her. "Esme!" she called up the stairs again, but to no avail. She returned to the man in the study, who had opened his coat and was pressing tenderly on his ribs.

"I might need a bit more ice," he smiled wanly. He looked to be about 60, if she had to guess. A little old for a field agent, maybe, but not unheard of. Her parents had just retired from field work a few years ago, and she suspected that they still took on low-risk missions from time to time.

"What happened to you, Niall? Shouldn't we get you to hospital?" She handed him the ice and he placed it gingerly on his swollen lip.

"Priorities, dear girl." He attempted to smile, but winced instead. "Are you ... of the Order?"

"I know of the Aegis Order, of course, but I work with the research and development side rather than Aegis Secundus. I don't have much inclination toward field work. I'm a physicist."

Niall's brows twitched. "Ah, I see. Well, I think the first business we should attend to is to reach out to the Order so I can ... report on my mission."

Eliza suspected that meant that he had an artifact in his possession which he needed to turn over to the Order for protection. "How dangerous is the artifact?" she asked.

Startled by her directness, he paused, assessing her. Surely a daughter of the Wrens was trustworthy. "Potentially quite dangerous if someone managed to weaponize it," he answered.

"So we need to get you to London, then," she decided. "Let me find my sister. I can't take off without letting her know what's happening. Then we'll get you to the Chapter House."

Niall nodded, his shoulders unknotting. He'd really dodged danger this time. Probably he should retire and leave this stuff to the young ones. Field work wasn't as fun as it used to be.

Esme pinched the charcoal between her fingers as she pictured her mother's face. She often sketched Mother, and she'd recently seen a photo of her parents on their wedding day. It was an over-the-shoulder shot of her father, but the look on her mother's face was one she'd never seen before. *The pure adoration of the young and hopeful,* Esme thought, *their whole lives ahead of them.*

Mother and Father still loved each other, of course, but this face ... this young woman had existed before Esme had been born. She wondered if this bride still lived somewhere inside of Beatrice.

She drew the familiar curve of her mother's face as meditation music flowed through her earbuds. That first line was always her favorite.

Her mother was the most beautiful woman in the world.

She lifted the charcoal to draw the hairline when the feeling seized her. She gasped as her vision became obscured by phantasmic black cloth. She could feel the charcoal's downward motion, increasingly frenetic and sharp. A sense of despair filled her and whispering voices moaned in her ears, drowning out the gentle tones of the music. Her left hand clutched the sketchpad and her right moved of its own volition, even as tears coursed down her cheeks.

Esme was overwhelmed with emotions that did not belong to her. The agony of it poured through her into the art her blinded hand was creating. Then, as suddenly as it began, the wave passed, and the charcoal slipped from her fingers. She began trembling, sliding from the chair in the moonlit garden, collapsing in a heap on the lawn.

She awakened to the sense of being shaken. "Esme! Dammit, Esme!" Eliza's voice pierced the darkness as the earbuds fell out of Esme's ears. She opened her eyes to see her older sister's face, brows knitted with concern.

"I .. I'm alright," Esme sputtered. "It was just ... you know ..."

"You haven't had one of these episodes in a while." Eliza breathed a sigh of relief. "Here, sit up slowly till the dizziness passes."

These artistic *episodes*, as Eliza called them, happened from time to time, and at first their parents had taken Esme to have a full neurological examination. It was only after they were assured that there was nothing medically wrong with her that they'd begun writing the spells off to her artistic temperament.

"Really, Liza, I'm fine. Sorry to have worried you."

"I was calling and couldn't find you. You sure you're alright?"

"Aces." The younger sister smiled, her blue-gray eyes crinkling up at the corners.

"Okay then. Listen, there's an Order agent in the study."

Esme sat up straighter. "Here? Why? Are Mother and Father okay?"

Eliza patted her sister's hand. "Nothing like that. He came for Sanctuary."

"Here?" Esme repeated.

"Yeah, I guess he knows our parents. Anyhow, I need to get him into the city, and ..."

"I'm coming with you," Esme declared, making a wobbly attempt at standing.

"I'm not sure you should, Ez. You were just ..."

"Nonsense. That's more reason not to leave me alone than it is not to take me. I'm coming."

"Okay, okay, come on, then." Eliza put her hand under Esme's right elbow and led her inside.

From the front of the house, they heard a door slam. "What in the world?" Eliza began, leaning Esme against the sliding glass door frame and rushing toward the study.

The sight that met her eyes was a horror. A dark stain spread across Niall's shirt and he spasmed, choking up blood.

Eliza cried out and leapt into action, trying to staunch the bleeding in the chest wound with direct pressure, but as Niall's life ran through her fingers, she realized it was futile. She wouldn't be able to save him.

"The Veil ..." he choked. "They took it ..." Niall grabbed Eliza's hand and pressed a scrap of black lace into her bloody palm. "You must ..." His body seized and then went still.

Eliza's eyes filled with tears, and she fought back the panic, knowing that there were immediate actions she needed to take. A gasp from behind her told her that Esme had made her way to the study.

"We need to ... the Order ..." Eliza couldn't get the words to come out coherently as she turned toward her sister.

"They told me," Esme sobbed. "They said ..."

"Who did?" Eliza stared at Esme's haunted expression.

"The whispers. They said ..." Esme found herself unable to finish. Instead, she held up her left hand, still clutching her sketchbook.

Unlike Esme's usual flowing style, the charcoal lines were sharp, deliberate, almost violent in their intensity.

Lines forming the unmistakable image of a woman's face veiled in black, screaming.

2

MURDER IN THE NEST

"We have to call the police," Eliza said, checking dark corners, looking to make sure whoever had entered and violated the sanctuary of the Wren's Nest didn't linger, waiting to strike again.

Esme paced the length of the carpet runner behind the sofa, her arms crossed, a thumbnail between her teeth as she fretted about what to do. "We can't call the police," she said. "Father said to contact Aegis Secundus if there was a problem."

"I work for the Order, albeit just the R&D branch," Eliza snapped, then softened her tone, seeing the worry in her sister's face. "I'll call the Proctor. I have his number." She took out her phone and dialed the number, putting the phone on speaker.

A rumble of thunder shook the house at the same moment the phone clicked. "Proctor Services."

"My name is Eliza Wren," she began, trying to formulate a rational thought in her mind. "We need assistance. An agent came to the house seeking Sanctuary."

"Dr. Wren, you're not authorized to provide ..."

"Eliza ..." Esme called her name, but Eliza turned her back on the room, trying to get through this phone call.

"I know," she said. "He came looking for my parents, but they're on holiday in Spain."

"Dr. Wren, you are not authorized to ..."

"Someone came into our house and killed him," she said. "He had an artifact, something he said was potentially dangerous in the wrong hands."

"Eliza..."

"In a minute, Esme ..."

There was a long silence on the other end of the phone. "One moment." The line clicked.

"Dr. Wren, this is Father Thomas Whittaker. Is the Sanctuary secure?"

"I ..." she glanced over at the front door that stood ajar. Rain fell in sheets beyond the covered portico. Across the expansive lawn, the wrought iron gates that allowed access to the drive were thrown open. Lightning flashed across the tops of the trees and the rain intensified. "No."

"Eliza..."

"Then you are not safe there," he said. "Take pictures of the area where he was killed. Multiple pictures, Dr. Wren. Collect your sister, and bring anything that you find in Niall Roth's possession to the Sanctum Sangrael."

"What? Where is that?"

"Your father hasn't told you the emergency plans?"

"No," she said. "I knew enough to call the Proctor. That's it."

"Can you get to Canterbury Cathedral?"

"Eliza!" Esme finally had enough. She stomped her foot on the hardwood and raised her pitch, knowing her sister was sensitive to such noises. Eliza turned, her attention going to the mirror over the mantel.

"We can be there in an hour." She hung up the phone and stuck it in her pocket as she came back into the living room. The mirror was cracked, and a symbol had been sketched by a hurried hand. The glyph was one Eliza recognized. The Covenant. "Esme, go pack a bag. Gather only what you need. We have to leave. We're not safe here."

"What about Faraday?"

"Don't worry about the cat!" Eliza snapped, studying the room with a trained eye. She took her phone back out and began snapping a series of pictures, including the mirror. She went to the man laying on the floor and snapped a few pictures of him before taking a pen from her jacket pocket and using it to probe into his pockets to see if he carried anything that might explain what had happened here. She spotted the glint of lightning reflected on something beneath the edge of his vest. Using the pen, she lifted the gold chain, and the pendant of Saint Christopher dangled from it.

Eliza's heart sank. "O Lord of Mercy, receive the soul of our fallen brother. Receive his soul for he was Your faithful servant and our brave companion. Saint Christopher, guide him across the threshold to glory, as You once bore Christ upon Your shoulders," Eliza prayed. "Deliver him safely to his rest. Let light perpetual shine upon him and grant him peace."

"Amen." Esme came in carrying her overnight bag. It was full to overflowing, her sketch pads and chalks not forgotten in her panic.

"Lock the doors," Eliza stood, crossing herself. She took a few more pictures as Esme obeyed her instructions. "Grab his bag and any belongings you can see, but don't touch anything else. I'll go grab a few things and meet you in the garage. We'll take the Bentley."

Esme's eyes flashed like she might protest.

"Father will understand."

Eliza watched her rearview mirrors as she drove through the blinding rain. It was as dark as any November night could ever be, except for the infrequent flashes of lightning. Esme sat in the seat next to her, clutching the cat she refused to leave behind. Faraday was Eliza's cat, but Esme loved him just as much as her sister did. The old silver-taupe tabby cat had dusty charcoal stripes and bright amber eyes. The light from the dashboard made his fur shimmer like stardust. Eliza noticed the cat gazing up at her, watching her. He was always two steps ahead of her, and sensed what she was thinking. Esme petted him absent mindedly, and he slow-blinked, as if none of this upset him.

"Should we call Father?" Esme said, startling Eliza as she drove.

"No," Eliza said. "Father Whittaker will know what to do."

"But can we trust him?"

"He's the Proctor. Why shouldn't we trust him?"

"Have you ever met him?"

"Not that I recall," Eliza said. "But that doesn't mean anything."

"I don't like it," Esme rocked the cat with renewed vigor. "Not one bit."

"We'll have to trust him," Eliza said. "We have nothing to go on but faith."

"Do you suppose that poor man in the living room had faith in us to protect him?"

"He had enough faith to come to the Wren Manor. He didn't know our parents were on holiday."

"And we failed him," Esme said, her voice faint.

Those words resounded in Eliza's ears for the remainder of the drive. Her phone chirped, startling her. Esme took it and read the message, allowing her sister to keep her attention on the road. "It's an address."

"Who is it from?"

"The caller ID says, *The Proctor*."

"Pull it up on the GPS," Eliza said.

The address led them to Canterbury Cathedral Lodge Hotel. The priest stood on the curb by the valet station when they pulled up, his umbrella protecting him from the deluge that buffeted the area. The heavy fog blocked the cathedral from view, but Eliza knew it was behind the guest house. The priest held the umbrella for Esme, then came around and collected Eliza. Once under the protection of the building, he went to the valet and instructed him to park the car out of sight.

"Why the change of venue?" Eliza asked as they stood inside the lobby. Her braid was soaked and rain water dripped over her shoulder, darkening the front of her jumper.

"Not here," he said, fishing an electronic key card from the pocket of his hassock. "Upstairs." The girls fell in behind him and no one spoke until they were safely behind a locked door on the second floor.

The room smelled musty and damp. The ghosts of old cigarettes found their way to Eliza's sensitive pallet. The priest scuttled about, checking for wiretaps and hidden monitoring devices while the girls watched him. Esme reached over and took her sister's hand as the priest came back and looked up at Eliza. She wasn't overly tall for a woman, but then, he wasn't overly tall for a man either. "Show me the pictures," he commanded with a gentle tone.

Eliza took out her phone and pulled up the camera roll, handing it to him. He scrolled through them, and Eliza was certain she saw him blanch and knew which picture had gotten to him. "No, not Niall ..." the cry from his throat was so faint it was almost imperceptive.

"Was he a friend?" Eliza asked.

"I recruited him," Father Whittaker said. "As his father recruited me."

"I'm sorry for your loss," Esme muttered, glancing at Eliza, swallowing hard.

"I've left a message for your parents," the priest told them, scrolling to the next photo. "There's no need for them to come home. We'll take care of everything, of course."

"We're both adults," Eliza pointed out. "We can manage ..."

"You'll stay here," the priest said. "Until the Order can arrange for your arrival to the Grand Aegis."

"Excuse me?" Eliza's eyelid twitched. She reached up and pushed her glasses back up the bridge of her nose.

"You've been working for our R&D Department for how long, Dr. Wren?"

"Almost a year," Eliza said.

"I've seen your papers," he said. "Brilliant work. You've passed every test we've given you. Both of you. It's time."

"For what?" Esme asked.

"For you to learn your true identity."

3

TWO TURTLE DOVES

"I don't like it," Esme continued as she repeatedly rubbed her hands down the thighs of her jeans as though ridding herself of the last vestiges of charcoal on her palms. "What did he mean, they've been testing us for years? I work in the gift shop at Hever Castle, for heaven's sake. What's he been testing? My ability to make change?"

"I don't know what he means, Ez." Eliza was tired all the way into her bones, but she knew she couldn't have slept if she wanted to. Every time she closed her eyes, all she could see was the light leaving Niall's eyes. She jammed her hands into her jacket pockets and started when her left thumb ran over something rough. She pulled it out and found herself staring at the scrap of the Veil that Niall had given her.

Out of nowhere, a shrill scream ripped through the air, and Eliza's hands flew up to cover her ears. "What is *that*?"

"What's what?" Esme asked, leaping to her feet and throwing herself in front of her sister, as if to shield her from an invisible attacker. She scanned the corners of the room, then turned back to Eliza. "What did you hear?"

Eliza slowly lowered her hands, the sound gone and only its memory remaining. "You didn't hear that screaming? It sounded like it was right next to my head!"

"No, I didn't hear a thing. I just saw you react."

"I ... I ... maybe I imagined it." How could Esme not have heard?

"Imagination doesn't hurt your ears," Esme pointed out. "Whatever you heard was just for you." Her eyes were earnest, not a shred of doubt. Eliza wished she felt as certain.

"It must've been in my head. It's been a stressful night. Hearing voices is your thing, not mine." She meant for it to be a joke, but it came out sounding snarky. "Sorry, Ez. I didn't mean it like that."

"I know you didn't, and you're not wrong. I *do* hear things others don't. That's why I know the difference between what's imagined and what isn't. It *was* in your head, but not the way you meant. Someone was ..." Esme's explanation was interrupted by a knock on their hotel room door.

Eliza slipped the lace back into her pocket and put her eye to the peephole before opening the door. "Father Whittaker."

"Sorry to keep you waiting, ladies, but the Grand Aegis has just arrived. Will you come with me, please?" He turned down the hallway, expecting them to follow. The women grabbed their purses and jogged after him.

Father Whittaker led them through the darkened streets around the east side of the cathedral and past a set of crumbling archways, echoes of the massive church's former glory. He approached a stone building half-overgrown with ivy that was just starting to wither in preparation for its winter sleep. The side door to the building might have been as old as the cathedral itself, as it tapered up into the same graceful Gothic arch seen in so much of the church's architecture. The priest knocked three times, hesitated, then knocked again. The door swung open with a soft creak.

"Dr. Wren, nice to see you." A woman in a crisp white blouse and grey slacks nodded at Eliza.

"Charmaine? I didn't expect to see you here." Charmaine was an administrative assistant within the Aegis Foundation's higher ranks, and Eliza had met her at a couple of company functions. "I thought you worked in ... London." She suddenly realized that she had no real idea of what Charmaine's role was within Aegis.

"Well, I go where they need me. Order, Secundus, Foundation ... everyone needs logistics, don't they?"

"I guess so."

"C'mon in. The boss is eager to see you." Charmaine ushered the sisters into a drawing room where a fire burned merrily in the hearth. "I'll be right back."

"Have you ever met the Grand Aegis?" Esme asked.

"A couple of times," Eliza answered. "One when we were kids, right after the car accident. He came to talk to our parents when we were at the hospital. And then I met him again when I started working for Aegis. He came by and chatted me up at the research lab. I was pretty surprised at that, actually, but I assume it had to be because of Mother and Father."

"So you were only seven the first time? How do you remember that?"

"Solan Virell makes an impression. You'll see." Eliza stood in front of the hearth, her arms crossed and her brow furrowed.

Esme seated herself on the window seat and pressed her cheek against the glass, watching the dark sky just as a spattering of rain, an afterthought of the earlier storm, pelted against the pane.

After a moment, Charmaine stepped back into the room, then stepped aside to let the Grand Aegis make his entrance.

Eliza hadn't been kidding about him making an impression. He was lean and imposing, more so than his six-foot frame would merit on another man. His brown hair, slicked back and bound into a tight knot at the base of his neck, was greying at the temples, but very little else about him gave any indication of his age. He appeared to be mid-40s, but there were rumors that he was much, much older. His impeccable navy blue suit looked posh, but if the light caught it just right, the shimmer of silvery runes could be glimpsed around the jacket's cuffs.

His eyes lighted on the older sister first. "Eliza," he smiled. "Lovely to see you again, despite the circumstances. You've certainly grown since we first met."

"And you haven't aged a day," she replied. "Quite unsettling, actually."

He chuckled, a throaty and deep rumble, and Charmaine slipped out the door through which they'd entered. "Good genes. Or good skin care. Hard to say." He turned to Esme. "And you must be Esme Wren."

"I must. You know our parents?"

"I know them well, though we haven't always seen eye to eye on some matters. I think, though, that under the circumstances, the Order needs to share some information with you. I told Simon and Beatrice I'd agree to keeping these details secret, but given tonight's events, I believe I must override that decision."

"What's this all about, Aegis?" Eliza's jaw was set as though she expected bad news. What had their parents kept from them?

"Solan, please."

"What's all this about, *Solan*?"

"I suppose there's nothing for it other than to tell you directly. You know of your heritage, of course ..."

"That our *extremely distant* ancestor Christopher Wren founded the Order? Yes, of course." The last thing Eliza needed was a genealogy lesson. Her father had trumpeted their family history for as long as she could remember.

"And it's there that it all begins. There is a place for all of Sir Christopher's descendants at the Order, or in its outlying arms, as long as parents make a formal introduction of their offspring to whoever holds the office of Grand Aegis before the children reach adulthood. That's more than just a tradition, but we'll get back to that presently."

"You mean I could have been working at the Foundation with Eliza?" Esme piped up.

"You could, indeed, if you ever showed any interest in doing so. Your parents were under the impression you were content to pursue your art and work outside the Order."

"I guess I never really thought about it." Esme was a little disappointed that no one had ever approached her with an alternative, but on the other hand, she wasn't sure she would have accepted a different path anyway. Perhaps her parents knew best.

"At any rate, the two of you have a somewhat more complicated history with us. Eliza, do you remember when we first met?"

"Of course. You came to the hospital after my family had that car accident. We were waiting for Esme's tests to come back since she had wiggled out of her car seat and hit her head."

"Just so. *And do you remember how young Esme felt after that accident?*"

Eliza didn't understand how any of this was connected to the murder that had just occurred in their study at home. "The doctors said she was fine. And about a month later, she started having her episodes, usually while she was drawing or playing with clay. Our parents thought maybe she had lingering head trauma, but the doctors said no."

"Marvelous memory, Eliza. Esme, my dear, do you recognize this?" Solan produced a sketch from the inner pocket of his jacket and handed it to her.

Esme studied the picture. It was done in heavy-handed crayon, a jumbled drawing that, at first, made no sense. A tree, lots of birds, lots of people

... "Oh, I know what this is!" she exclaimed after a moment. "It's 'The 12 Days of Christmas!' Look ... there are seven swans, and nine ladies dancing ... but I don't remember drawing it. I signed it, so I must have, but I have no memory of it." As she held the drawing, the voices gathered around her, whispering as they so often did. She began humming the Christmas carol, and the voices quieted.

"I remember when you drew this," Eliza said. "It was the first time you had an episode. You were five. I was in the garden with you, and you started mumbling and drawing like a girl possessed, and I couldn't get you to respond to me, so I went and got Mother. It was terrifying, if I'm honest. Then when you finished, you just went to sleep right there on the lawn. When you woke up for dinner, you didn't remember a thing about it."

"Oh ..." Esme was at a loss for what to say. She felt as though she should apologize.

"It was then that we realized that Esme had *gifts*," Solan added. "Once your parents ruled out brain damage," he smiled indulgently at Esme as though they shared an inside joke, "they brought the drawing to the Order. You drew parts of this image over and over for years, you know. I have all of those sketches."

"Why?" Esme asked, confused. "Why would you care if I drew pictures of a Christmas song?"

"Eliza, do you remember what Esme was mumbling while she drew?"

Eliza had grown very still. "I do."

Esme spun to look at her sister, alarmed by the guarded tone in her voice. "What did I say, Liza?"

"You kept repeating, 'It all begins with blood in the nest.'" Eliza pointed to the picture Esme held, where two birds sat in a nest on one branch of the tree. There were bold streaks of red crayon through the brown of the nest's twigs.

"Yes, indeed." Solan said. "And so it has. Now it's time for our two turtle doves to know what that means. Shall we sit? This might not be the kind of conversation you want to have standing up."

Eliza took the hint and settled into a comfortable wing chair close to the window bench where Esme had crossed her legs like a child in primary school ready for a story.

Solan nodded and sat on the loveseat that faced the fire, but angled his body so that he was looking at the sisters. "You may be wondering why your parents thought it necessary to bring a child's drawing to the attention of the Order." He paused, and Esme nodded while Eliza pressed her lips tightly together, girding herself for bad news. It was always bad news when people told you to sit.

"Doesn't everyone pin their children's art work to the breakroom fridge?" Eliza asked. "Though I would argue my sister's work is more exceptional than most. Perhaps framed in the hallway would be better."

Solan's lip twitched, though whether in a smile or a frown was unclear. "Many of the people in your bloodline have gifts. Yours, Eliza, is your brilliant mind and facility with languages, and — unless I miss my guess — there will be others that emerge over time. Your brother Elias, rest his soul, could read mathematical patterns like music, which made him an ideal cryptographer. He was quite good at it, you know. I remember him fondly." The Grand Aegis bowed his head.

Esme's eyes narrowed. "People always assume ..." Her voice trailed off.

Solan continued as if she hadn't spoken. "His was a tremendous loss, and his service to the Order will never be forgotten. He died defending what he believed in. And Esme, as soon as your parents realized that your artistic trances were natural to you and not the cause of trauma, they started to take much closer looks at your work. We've got quite a collection of your sketches in the archives, my dear."

"I'm not sure if I should be flattered or freaked out," Esme commented, a sliver of anger in her voice. She didn't like it when people assumed Elias was dead. A body had never been recovered, after all.

"Probably a bit of both," Solan answered with a soft chuckle. "Some of your artwork is laced with prophecy, you see. And this crayon drawing was the first prophecy that the Universe fed you."

"What does that mean?" Eliza's voice had an edge to it, and she felt the urge to tell the Grand Aegis to leave her sister out of it … whatever *it* was.

"You hear things in your trances, isn't that right, Esme?"

"Yes, whispers mostly. But sometimes they don't make words, or the words don't make sense. Sometimes I can't remember what they said."

"Ah, but those whispers often direct what you draw, yes?"

"Well, yes, but what does that have to do with Christmas?" She picked at a fleck of paint on her shirt.

"In itself, nothing. But when your parents studied this drawing more closely, your mother realized that it paired with something she'd read in her studies at the Aegis archives. I've brought you a copy." He fished yet another paper out of his inner pocket and handed it to Eliza. Esme scooted closer and read over her shoulder.

The First stands alone, cloaked in fruit and root.
Find the tree whose fruit bears seeds in threes.
The doves fly not apart, nor tethered—they are the bond.
One sees the path, the other shields it.
Three queens of knowledge—earth, air, fire—
Nested beneath a shattered dome.
Voices from the quarters, carried on wind in whispers
Heed them, for they sing of betrayal.
Bound in circles, five forged by fire
When worn, they silence truth and amplify lies.

The eggs are not unborn, but buried—six vaults, six keys.

Guarded by feather and fang.

Grace on the surface, but beneath—feral motion.

The seventh swims alone, and knows.

Shepherds in plain garb, drawing truth from shadow.

But not all maids serve the same master.

A masquerade of grace hides a choreography of death.

The ninth wears crimson beneath white.

The leap is one of faith.

Ten will fall before the First is restored.

The tune is a call to arms.

Eleven notes echo through time.

Only the true heir can hear them.

The rhythm signals war.

When the twelve fall silent, the final curse awakens.

"This is gibberish," Eliza grumbled. "I mean, I see where you'd find parallels to 'The 12 Days of Christmas, but ...'" Even as she said it, she knew that the metaphors in the poem had deeper implications. They were on a precipice, and if they leapt forward, their lives would never be the same.

"It's us!" Esme interrupted, who clearly didn't share Eliza's sense of dread. "We're the turtle doves!"

Solan gave Esme an indulgent look that reminded Eliza of one that a teacher might give a star pupil. "We believe that you are, yes."

"Okay, let's say that's true. What about the rest of it then?" Eliza pushed.

"To be completely honest, we haven't figured out the significance of all of it. The poem is nearly three hundred years old and was translated from Portuguese. You can see why it stood out as odd right away, since the carol we know now didn't appear until 1780. The children's book in which it was first published was, in point of fact, a code to Aegis Order members, who were still staying very much out of the public eye back then. Our fair country didn't have the finest historical record of treating mystics well, you know.

"In any case, we do have some theories. We believe the *shattered dome* refers to St. Paul's, the six refer to six cursed Fabergé eggs which are kept in six separate Order vaults, but most importantly, we think we know what the *First* refers to."

"And what's that?" The edge had slipped out of Eliza's voice, her curiosity having won out over her risk aversion.

"When Sir Christopher Wren formed the Order back in the late 17th century, he kept a book listing and detailing artifacts which held powerful enchantments ... powerful enough that they were too dangerous to be left floating around the world wreaking havoc, particularly if unsavory characters got hold of them. In his journals, he referred to this book as the First Manifest ... in entries after 1685, he simply called it Manifest."

"Why did he change the title?" Esme asked, swept up in Solan's story.

"Because in 1685, the Covenant ...which had been seeking many of these artifacts so that they could find ways to use their power ... raided your ancestor's secret study and attempted to steal the book and any other relics they could find. They did make off with a few items, but fortunately, Sir Christopher had the room booby trapped, so he was able to escape and minimize the loss."

"Did they take the Manifest?" Eliza leaned forward, now drawn into the tale as well.

"Ah, that's the best part of the story! According to Sir Christopher, the Manifest developed — shall we say — a mind of its own over the years. Perhaps because of its constant exposure to magical objects, perhaps something else. But when it felt threatened, it vanished. It was Sir Christopher's belief that it took itself to a place of safety."

"So no one has seen it in more than three centuries?" Esme didn't have time to work out the exact math, which Elias would have calculated instantly.

"Both the Order and the Covenant have searched for it, of course. But it was only successfully located once, in 1904 in Edinburgh Castle of all places. An Order agent named Cecil Ashcroft was able to get his hands on it and took it back to his home in Newcastle. He contacted the Order's main chapter in London, and an agent named Thomas Swann was sent to retrieve the book and return it to St. Paul's."

"Swann!" Esme cried. "Like the seven swans!"

"Swann indeed. He was a respected member of the Order, but had, in fact, gone rogue and was working for the Covenant. When he arrived at the Ashcroft home, we don't know precisely what tipped Cecil off, but there was a struggle. Cecil's wife Eleanor rushed downstairs when she heard the commotion, and arrived just in time to see her husband brutally beaten to death. It is said that when Swann reached for the Manifest, it disappeared before his eyes. Poor Mrs. Ashcroft promptly fainted, and when she awoke, she was left with an open door and the body of her dear husband."

"Oh, that's just horrible!" Esme's eyes were full of tears. "That poor woman."

"Yes, I'm afraid Eleanor went quite mad. After Cecil's death, she donned a mourning veil, and never took it off for as long as she lived. She rarely spoke, only wailed, wept, and even screamed for the rest of her life."

"Wait." Realization began to dawn on Eliza, her quick mind making connections between the day's events and Solan's story. "The veil ... was it ..."

"Cursed? Oh, quite so. Why do you ask, Eliza?"

She drew the scrap of lace from her pocket and showed it to Solan. "I think that Niall had it, and that whoever killed him took it."

Solan gasped. "Oh, my dear girl ... you touched it with your bare hand? Charmaine," he called urgently, "I need a capture bag — NOW!"

Charmaine hustled in with an iridescent blue baggie in her hand. Her eyes grew wide when she saw what was in Eliza's outstretched palm. Wordlessly, she held the baggie open while Eliza dropped the fragment inside. Then she sealed the bag shut and hurried from the room.

"Is Eliza cursed?" Esme's eyes were desperate.

"There may have been some contamination, but hopefully it was minimal. Eliza, you must let the Order know immediately if you begin feeling inexplicable depression or dread." He sighed and ran his hand down his bronzed face. "I'm afraid this creates a heightened sense of urgency."

"I'm going to need an explanation of what that means. Immediately." Eliza's heart was pounding. She was a *physicist*, for heaven's sake. She didn't meddle in the mystical side of Aegis for a reason.

"The fact that you've had direct contact with the Mourning Veil, which is one of the objects our agents have been after for years incidentally, means that you'll have a heightened insight as to its whereabouts. Its energy will be drawn to you, and given the circumstances around how you came to touch a piece of it, I suspect the violence connected with its creation and the violence of the past few hours will strengthen its power. You are our best chance of recovering the Veil and containing its magic. If we can get it into a containment vault, it will lose any power over you and anyone else who has been affected by it."

"So you're telling us that we need to search for the Veil?" Eliza stammered. "We aren't field agents."

"I don't even work for the Order," Esme protested.

"I'm afraid you do now," Solan shook his head. "That was actually why I came here to meet you. 'It all begins with blood in the nest.' Those were Esme's words. When Niall was murdered in the Wren's Nest, the prophecy ball had started rolling, as it were. I came to you to enlist you, our turtle doves, to find the Manifest. We believe that is what the poem is saying in the first two lines: *The First stands alone, cloaked in fruit and root. / Find the tree whose fruit bears seeds in threes.* You are temporal twins, are you not?"

"Come again?" Eliza asked.

"He means our birthdays!" Esme stood, her eyes shining. "We were both born on March 3rd, but two years apart!"

Solan nodded. "Precisely. You are descendants of the first Grand Aegis: Sir Christopher Wren himself. The Order has long suspected that the two of you would be the ones to recover the Manifest and return it to our safekeeping. There are many relics out there which are only known through the Manifest, and they could be doing untold damage to our world if they are in the wrong hands. This is the essence of the Order's mission. This is *your* destiny. And, it seems, you now have the added incentive to recover the Veil before it can cause you genuine harm."

"Why? What will it do to me?"

"It's hard to say for sure, as your exposure was limited, but it would not be unreasonable to say that your sanity may be at stake."

Eliza stared into the fire, but it was not the flames she saw. All she could picture was the screaming face in Esme's sketch, a warning from the Universe.

4

WHEN THE VOX SPEAKS

M aelis Varrow descended the spiral steps of the old observatory, her boots whispering against the stones that had been worn smooth by centuries of secrets. The *Sanctum Tenebris* lay beneath a ruined abbey that once protected the Brides of Christ through the onslaught of Viking raids, the slaughter by Roman legions, and the bombings by German during the Blitz. Her private chambers were guarded by ancient symbols, older than language, burned into the walls with blood and iron.

Candles flickered to life as she entered, reacting to her presence. Shadows coiled like breath around shelves of ancient scrolls, relics suspended in glass, and tomes bound by human hide. In the heart of the room, the Veil lay unfurled atop a black marble altar, draped like a fallen banner, its threads humming with dormant power.

She reached out, reverently, and brushed her fingers along its edge. Such action might be dangerous for others, but not for the High Seer of the Covenant. Her magic was strong enough to protect her from any force bound into the relic. The silk was impossibly fine, tatted not for the living but for those who passed between worlds.

Then her hand stilled.

A seam, subtle but undeniable, had been severed, torn from the corner. It was only a fragment that was missing, but the frayed edges unraveled and magic crackled from the artifact, leaking, bleeding.

"Impossible," she whispered, voice razor thin.

She turned as the scribe came down the stairs. "This was recovered from the Wren Estate?" she demanded.

The wiry woman, hunched to the wall, fearing the wrath of the High Seer. "It was found as you see it now, Matriarch. The Warden reports there was ... *resistance*."

Maelis turned back to the Veil, worries racing through her mind like eels swarming in a shallow pool. The Veil, even its fragments, would have power. The piece would want to be reunited. Worse, the Veil might be awakened.

Her fingers curled into a fist. "Bring me the Warden who failed me. Send another to find the missing fragment," she murmured, "before they remember how to use it!"

And deep in the marble beneath her feet, something shifted, something that had been waiting a very long time. The air rippled as the scribe made a hasty retreat up the winding staircase. Her attention returned to the Veil, bleeding magic on the table. Shimmers of its life force reminded her of its power. Without the missing piece, the Veil would continue to hemorrhage. Time was of the essence.

"When the Vox summons, I answer," the Warden bowed before her upon reaching the bottom of the staircase. "How may I serve you?"

"You had one charge, Warden," she whispered to the echoing air. "And now we bleed because of your failure."

"But," he sputtered, dropping to one knee, his face to the floor in reverence.

"You knelt before the Chorus and swore your hands were steady. You were to bring me the Veil, the whole Veil."

"There was interference. The Aegis..."

"Aegis Secundus is a rotted tooth with no root. Your missive was to bring me the Veil at any cost. Dr. Wren is an old man and his wife, a crone. You vowed your strength before the Chorus and yet you failed me?"

"Dr. Wren wasn't there," the Warden cowered. "Nor was his wife."

"Who has the fragment of my Veil?" Maelis demanded.

"The Agent of the Order fell to my blade, Matriarch. But the daughters ... the oldest came in just as I grabbed the Veil. I didn't realize it was torn. Not until I returned it to the Sanctum."

"You are relieved," she said, coldly. "The Penumbra will escort you to the Ashwright." The Warden flinched, but did not protest. "There you will remain until the Chorus convenes. If the relic is not retrieved before the next lunar gate, you will be offered as a tithe." He tried to speak — perhaps to beg, perhaps to curse — but the twin shadows of the Penumbra were already at his shoulders, as silent as dusk.

Maelis turned away. "Pray that the fragment is found before the world forgets your name."

The *Sanctum Tenebris* was a cold deep chamber beyond the walls of the abbey. It was erected beneath the cemetery — unconsecrated ground. Above the seven-sided table, the chandelier of emberglass flickered, its glow cast shifting sigils on a vaulted ceiling. The chamber was redolent of patchouli, parchment and phosphor.

The Councilors of Tenebras, Maelis's inner circle, and each a master of their own domain, took their places.

The Curator accepted the offering she brought. He studied it with a wizened old eye, cloudy with visions of the future and memories of the past. "This is of no use to us," the ancient keeper of relics said.

"The Warden allowed a fragment to remain in the hands of the Wren children. My visions tell me the eldest daughter has been touched by the fragment." She turned to the Ashwright. "I have sentenced the Warden who failed into your custody. He will pay for his carelessness."

"Better turn the Warden into a lesson," the Ashwright, master of punishments and rites of atonement, spoke firmly, his deep voice echoing in the rafters. "Bleed him in the Plaza of Ash. Let the Covenant know the cost of error."

The Sabelton, cloaked in black, rose. "Fear sharpens loyalty. But discretion is sharper still. Quiet punishment, loud redemption, if I may be so bold, High Seer."

"Until the Chorus convenes, there is to be no harm to him. His tormented mind will do our work for us. If the fragment is not returned by the lunar gate, then he will pay in blood."

"A just decision," the Sableton acquiesced and sat back down.

If the Ashwright felt denied of his duties, he didn't show it. "When the Vox speaks, I listen," the Ashwright said with a nod.

Nyxander, the High Ritualist, came to Maelis' side, his hand brushing hers as if to calm her. "Binder? Can the veil be mended? If only temporarily?" he asked.

"That is not within my power," the Binder said. "If this were a conflict between factions, or some oath that might have been broken, I would have the power to intervene. Perhaps the Hollowed Seer has such power?"

The Hollowed Seer, a frail old woman with her eyes bound, sat at the right hand of the High Seer. Despite the wrappings, her eyes were forever bleeding. She lifted her gnarled hands, reaching for the Veil. Nyxander took it, handing it to the crone.

She took in a deep breath and clutched the Veil to her chest, as if embracing the powers remaining within it. "The Veil breathes. Its severed piece draws storms. Two lights approach it — winged and weeping,"she said, her voice like wind through bone.

The Lexicant, decipherer of the sacred texts and linguistic puzzles, moved over the Hollowed Seer's shoulder to study the ripping glyphs on the surface of the lace. "The Veil can still be used until we recover the fragment," he said. "But it must be whole when the eclipse comes. You know what will happen if we fail."

Maelis narrowed her eyes. "Then we won't."

She stepped into the inner circle of the table, lifting her arms. "Let the Sableton send forth our Wardens to serve as our eyes and ears. Find the fragment of the Veil at any cost. Send our ghosts across the waters. I will not be mocked by children playing heroes."

An echoed response rose in the chamber. "When the Vox speaks, we listen."

Midnight had long since passed when Nyxander entered his Matriarch's chamber unbidden. Not even her handmaids had the pleasure to enter without the Matriarch's command, but he was pleased to find she bade them to prepare a late meal before sending them away. Two goblets sat by the ewer of wine. Her bed had been made, the draperies drawn back, telling him the Queen had not yet retired, and he was not too late to come to her service.

The High Seer's bath had been drawn and the copper tub sat near the fire. Maelis lay submerged to her collarbones, her raven hair coiled at the nape of her neck like a crown unbothered by rule.

Petals of the *lunavelle* blossoms floated atop the placid surface, their silvery hue casting glimmers in on her bare skin beneath the waters. Steam curled like fingers above the tub and the perfume of the flowers reminded him of crisp mountain air and something wild, like damp moss after the snowmelt. It reminded him of their first night together in the ruins of the ancient Gilnockie Tower, where they lay beneath an open sky, snow falling down on his naked back like icy kisses of the frost maidens.

He approached, letting his fingers trace the water's surface, disrupting the stillness and the petals. "Preparing to summon dreams of true love?" he whispered.

A wry smile spread across the High Seer's placid face, but her eyes did not open. "You are here, are you not?" She collected herself, donning the mask of betrayal, a role rehearsed in silence with truths her lover must not know. Not yet, anyway.

"Only if you'll have me," he said. "I feared the troubling news about the Veil might leave you sulking."

"Lunavelle is said to also soothe a restless soul," she said, opening her eyes, lifting her chin to take him in as he shrugged off his cloak.

"You tease," he said, gruffly. "Nothing short of having the full Veil in your grasp will soothe your soul, and we both know it."

Maelis sat up, the water sliding off her skin, while the petals clung to her flesh. "I am sure you have ways of making me forget my troubles, at least for a while." She reached for his hand, and used it to lift herself from the steaming waters. She drew his lips to hers. His whiskers buffeted her tender skin as he took her mouth, wrapping an arm around her supple body, drawing her into him. Their lips battled for authority as she welcomed his kisses, moaning her need for more.

"Tell me what you would have me do." He breathed the words onto the flesh of her neck.

"Take me, Nyx. As your Queen, I command thee."

"When the Vox speaks, I listen."

5

THE ARCHIVES

"I don't see why she has to carry it with her," Esme complained as Father Whittaker navigated the Order's company Audi through the outskirts of London. The rain was spitting against the windows, reflecting the mood of the drive.

"There are several reasons," the priest explained, his voice betraying the edge of impatience. "The Veil fragments are going to be drawn to each other, and that might manifest itself in any number of ways. Eliza has to be the one to carry it, since she's already been in contact with it, and it makes no sense to risk contaminating anyone else."

"He's right about that part," Eliza mumbled. The events of the past 24 hours were catching up with her. She was a light sleeper and had awakened during the night, thinking she'd heard Esme sobbing in her sleep. Upon investigation, her younger sister had been soundly unconscious. Eliza hadn't mentioned it to Esme, having written it off as stress from the evening's traumatic events.

What little sleep she had gotten had been punctuated by nightmarish images of Niall Roth's body bleeding all over her father's office.

"Even though we've placed it in a protective case, it may well be strong enough to influence her to follow the pull to the rest of the Veil," Father Whittaker continued. "Obviously, we need to locate the rest of the Veil, so should that happen, you'd inform us immediately and follow where the pull leads you. But be careful, of course. We wouldn't want you engaging any of the Covenant. Clearly, they'd kill to possess this relic, and by now, they've realized that a part of it has been ripped away."

"See, that's where you're losing me," Esme griped. "We aren't trained as field agents, and you're putting us in danger. We're going to be a Covenant magnet."

"We're already in danger," Eliza sighed. "We're in the field whether we want to be or not. The Covenant came into our *house*, Ez. Well, our parents' house, anyway. We have to see this through." Her heart was breaking, and the life she'd built was crumbling around her ears. After Elias had disappeared a decade ago while on a mission, she'd held out hope that he'd return. But as year after year had passed, she'd had to force herself to accept the reality that he was probably dead at the hand of some Covenant Warden, just like Niall Roth. It was the whole reason she'd eschewed field work for research and development. She didn't want her family to mourn that way again. She turned her face toward the window so Esme wouldn't see the tear sliding down her cheek.

"Unfortunately, that's exactly right. But today's activities should be safe enough. I'm taking you to the Order's London Archives."

"Where Mother worked?" Esme doodled a bird on her hand with a ballpoint pen she'd found on the floor of the car.

"Yes, she was here often, as you know."

"Sometimes, when we were little, she'd bring us in with her and let us loose in the British Museum while she worked." Eliza wiped the tear away and tried to focus on the day ahead.

"It's a little different getting into the Archives than it once was. The contents of the British Library used to be housed in a section of the Museum, but they moved the documents to St. Pancras in 1997. You were quite small then," he added. "At any rate, a room full of documents was the perfect cover for an entrance to other rooms full of documents. Now, unfortunately, the entrance is in a posh gift shop." He shrugged off his moment of nostalgia. "At any rate, I think the best thing is for you two to research everything you can about the Veil. Perhaps you can get a better idea of how the Covenant might hope to use it. You won't be at risk in the Archives, at least."

"From your mouth to God's ears," Esme muttered as the great gates of the Museum came into view. "Where will you be?"

"I'm headed to St. Paul's. I need to file a report and make sure Niall's next of kin are notified. It's also the only place in the City of London where I can park. Just message me when you're ready to leave, and I'll come and get you and take you back to Canterbury."

He rolled to a stop outside the Museum, and the women jumped out of the car. The massive black iron gates stood open, giving a clear view of their destination. Eliza had always felt that the British Museum looked like a hybrid between a great palace and a Greek temple. Throughout her childhood, she had liked sitting in the courtyard, staring up at the elaborate frieze and Ionic columns and pretending that she was the goddess Athena, revered for her wisdom and cleverness. Now, though, she just wanted to get out of the rain.

The sisters hustled across the courtyard and up the great white steps toward the entrance. Once safely under the overhang, Esme shook herself like a wet dog while Eliza dropped a five-pound note in the large donation box.

"How is it that the entrance smells like sausage? It seems disrespectful somehow," Esme complained, eyeing the cafe at the bottom of the steps.

"Nothing for it," Eliza sighed. "Let's get in there."

They entered the building, and Esme grabbed her sister's hand as she looked at the Great Court, its white marble gleaming, even as the cloudy English day cast grey light through the glass ceiling.

"It never gets old, does it?" Esme asked dreamily. "This is my happy place."

Eliza chuckled despite her melancholy mood. "Every museum is your happy place. Come on, then."

They took a right and entered a gift shop that specialized in higher-end items, including fine jewelry and statuary. The clerk was assisting a middle-aged couple who appeared to be purchasing a bracelet.

"You know, since I started working at the Aegis Foundation, I've learned some interesting facts about this place," Eliza whispered. "There are at least half a dozen relics under the Order's protection that are actually on display in the main galleries. They're in cases, of course, but those cases have special security measures designed to dampen mystical ..." She stopped speaking abruptly as the couple thanked the clerk and walked toward the exit.

Once they were out of earshot, Esme excitedly bounced up to the counter. She'd been giddy at the notion of being able to give a passphrase that would grant them entrance to the secret vaults below.

"Um, hello," she chirped. The clerk gave Esme the smile that all retail employees master. "I wonder if you might be able to assist us? We're looking for a gift for Grendel's mother." The phrase had been a reference to the fact that the manuscript of *Beowulf* had once been housed in the collection that had now been moved to St. Pancras.

The clerk, a woman of perhaps 60 years with mousy blond hair, darted her eyes toward the door of the shop, and seeing that there were no customers on their way in, nodded formally to the sisters and straightened her posture, gaining her about two inches in height. "I've heard she's notoriously difficult to shop for. Follow me." She pressed against a wooden panel that led into a storeroom and the girls ducked inside. There was a keypad next to a metal door and the woman tapped in a six-digit code while whispering something Eliza couldn't hear. The door swung open and the clerk ushered them into a well-lit beige stairwell. "Down two floors, then left. You'll see the reception desk." She abruptly closed the heavy door and the girls found themselves alone.

"The air sings here," Esme murmured. "Do you hear it?"

"I don't know what that means, Ez. Maybe you're feeling the hum of the security system."

Esme responded by humming to herself and swaying gently from side to side, her eyes far away. Eliza took her by the arm and led her down the stairs.

The entryway to the Archives looked much like the most stereotypical of reception areas in every office building they'd ever been in, with the exception that there were no windows because they were two storeys underground. The assistant at the desk had been told to expect them, he said, and asked them to sit for a moment while he contacted the reading room administrator. They didn't have to wait long. In fewer than five minutes, an effusive and portly gentleman bustled into the reception area. He was quite out of breath.

"What a pleasure it is to have Wrens back in the Archives," he gushed. "I'm Randall Greaves, Senior Archivist, and I'm here to help you with anything you need." His waistcoat was rumpled and adorned with an anachronistic watch chain. He shook both of their hands heartily and then pushed his sliding glasses back up on his nose.

"Wonderful to meet you," Eliza greeted him. "Thank you for making time for us today."

"Making time? Ha!" the Archivist laughed, patting the watch pocket on his waistcoat. "If you only knew! Ha!" He hesitated, realizing that they weren't quite in on the joke. "Truth be told, I couldn't *wait* to meet with you. This is really quite a treat. I'm sorry for the circumstances, of course ... poor Niall. Best darts player I ever met." Randall paused for a moment and sniffed. "But I'm just the man to see when it comes to relic lore. Particularly about anything related to the Manifest." He began walking toward a large stone archway which led into the next room, and the girls followed.

"Well, we're here mostly about the Veil," Eliza began.

"Oh, they're not mutually exclusive, my dear. You can't learn about the Veil without learning about the Manifest."

"Why is that?"

"Oh, they're quite tied together, Dr. Wren. Are you familiar with the concept of *temporal bonding*?"

"You mean how relics that exist together in the same place and time can begin to have similar electrical signatures?"

"Oh, yes, ha! You're the physicist, of course. So you'd know about the electrical mumbo jumbo. Outside my area of expertise, that. But there's so much more to it! You see, the Manifest is a relic of not only great power, but *sentience*."

"Sentience?" Esme chimed in. "It's alive?"

"Well, not in the sense that most people understand life, of course. But it is rumored to have likes and dislikes, and of course, a strong sense of self-preservation." They arrived at a small, private conference room with a heavy wooden table with four chairs, and Randall gestured for the girls to sit. "The Manifest has made only three appearances since it first disappeared from Sir Christopher's vault in 1685. The first time was in Venice in the early 1700s. It was found in a monastery, but at the time the monks didn't realize what it was. They just knew they could not open it."

There was a shuffling from below the table, and a fluffy orange cat leapt up and plopped himself in the center, studying the visitors.

"Who's this?" Esme grinned, holding her hand out for the cat to sniff. "Do you smell Faraday?"

"This is Tiberius," Randall smiled. "He's really not supposed to be here, but I'm alone here a great deal, and he is marvelous company. Occasionally, he can detect if an item is cursed. Mostly he naps."

Tiberius gave a *rowr* and rubbed against Esme's elbow, then Eliza's. "I guess we pass muster." Eliza smiled in spite of her mood.

Randall scratched the feline's chin affectionately. "He's an absolute menace. Anyway, where was I? Oh, yes. The Manifest. It was in the private office of one of the clergy there who was trying to study it. He spent most of his time transcribing Bible verses, of course, and producing some beautifully illustrated pages. It was really more of a hobby at that point, since the printing press had already been invented and the monks weren't really producing illuminated manuscripts anymore, but ... oh, my, I've gotten off topic. Apologies. At any rate, it was rumored that any of the monks who worked at that desk to write letters or prayers or what-have-you, would be as eloquent as angels. But only when they worked at that desk, and only with a particular pen, as I recall. Eventually, this led to competition and discord in the monastery, because the members of the priesthood argued over whose turn it was, and then one day, the Manifest was simply gone. Possibly stolen, but more likely, it simply moved itself to another location. The pen disappeared shortly after, and one of the monks with it, so the theory is that Brother Whoever-he-was made off with the pen and changed his name."

"Perhaps he became a poet," Esme commented.

"Perhaps indeed, my dear, perhaps indeed. I've long suspected something of the sort. There wouldn't have been much point in selling it, as no one would have believed such a preposterous story, but ..."

"What does that have to do with the Veil?" Eliza was interested in the lore, but wished Randall would get to the point.

"Oh, everything! You see, the Manifest's energy *created a relic* as a result of its physical and temporal overlap with a perfectly ordinary pen. Sir Christopher had another item he claimed had been affected by the Manifest. A Futhark runestone, it was, with the character *Kenaz*, which is associated with fire. According to Sir Christopher's journal, it 'burns away lies and reveals the truth,' though we've never been able to test it."

"It's here?" Eliza's eyebrows arched.

"Indeed! It was part of our original collection. Initially, it had been part of a disturbingly accurate set of runes a seer might use, and that's why Sir Christopher had it. But it was in the vault with the Manifest for three or four years, and over that period of time, it developed other abilities. Sadly, Sir Christopher was not particularly specific about how he may have tested its properties."

"When did it appear next?" Esme asked.

"In the cabin of a merchant ship's captain on his way to America in 1847. The crew said that the captain had found it on one of his voyages and, superstitious man that he was, he kept it with his maps and charts. Said he considered it good luck and thought it was an angel's book, because human hands couldn't open it. The story goes that one time, this ship got hopelessly lost on a Transatlantic journey, and the crew feared that they would run out of food and water, tossed about as they'd been by storms and such. The captain and first mate prayed over the Manifest, hoping its angel would hear them. And then somehow, they were able to right themselves and found land within three days. They said the Manifest's angel guided the compass and brought the ship to safety. Then the next report of the Manifest that we have is when Cecil Ashcroft came up with it in Edinburgh."

"I think I'm beginning to see the pattern, but the Veil didn't sit in an office with the Manifest."

"Oh, not as such Dr. Wren," Randall leaned over the table, and his glasses began to slide down his nose again. He pushed them back up and continued. "But it may well have been in the house while Cecil Ashcroft had the Manifest in his possession."

"That seems an awfully random item to be affected. Why not a candlestick or handkerchief? Why not the silverware on the table?" Eliza asked.

"Ah, yes, indeed. Excellent question! But you are working under the assumption that time is linear. Cecil's murder caused a great energy disruption in that house. So much so that the Manifest moved itself before Thomas Swann could take possession of it. That energy settled into poor Eleanor Ashcroft and fueled her grief. And her grief was extra fuel for the Veil's magic."

"How much of this is fact, and how much is lore?" Eliza's scientific mind didn't like all the logical gaps.

Randall chortled and gave the table a slap. "Now that you mention it, about 50/50. But we do have some detailed documents on the Veil. I gathered them in anticipation of your visit. I presume you'd like to look those over?"

"Yes, please."

Randall rose from the table and slipped out of the room, returning a few minutes later with an acid-free folio full of old papers and two sets of white gloves.

"Please use the gloves when handling the documents. I've also brought some paper so you can take notes. I'll save you time and tell you not to take photos of the documents; the security measures here will cause the photos to look like giant lens flares. You helped work on that project, didn't you, Dr. Wren?"

"Some of the electrical research, yes, but I didn't develop the tech."

"Ah, still, top work. I'll leave you to it and check on you in a half hour, if that's all right? I have a cheese and pickle sandwich in my lunch, and it's calling my name."

"That would be wonderful. Thank you," Eliza nodded.

When he was gone, Esme grinned at Eliza. "Do you buy all that about the supposed relics?"

"I don't know, Ez. Stranger things than that have happened, believe me. Let's see what we can learn about the Veil." Without thinking, she reached into her shirt pocket and produced the scrap of black lace. Father Whittaker had placed it in a small, round, plastic container, similar to one a coin collector might use. "Something doesn't feel right, though. I don't think it's Randall; he seems genuine. But something is off. I feel like we're being watched."

"But there's no one here, Liza. Just you, me, Randall, and the receptionist. Oh, and Tiberius, but I think he's above board."

"I know, I know, Ez. But I just can't kick the feeling." She shook her head as though that might dispel the seeping paranoia. "Let's just learn what we can."

Unfortunately, there wasn't much, other than the lore Randall had already imparted. The only information they were able to add was from a series of reports from Eleanor's live-in caregiver Marie. The reports verified that Eleanor's face was never seen without the Veil after her husband's death, though she may have taken it off when she was alone. She had lived for eight years after the murder, and most of her waking hours were spent weeping. She had frequent nightmares about the murder and often woke up screaming. None of it seemed all that remarkable. They were nearly finished with the folio when Esme tapped her sister's arm.

"Hey, check this out. It's another one of Marie's reports to the doctor. But this one is a little different."

"Read it to me."

Esme took a deep breath, then began.

"Dr. Miller,

I write this letter with a sense of unease. Mistress Eleanor insisted that we visit the churchyard where Mr. Ashcroft was buried, which is something she has refused to do up until now, despite her mourning. I was concerned that she would be quite overcome, but I couldn't bear to deny her.

As we stood in the churchyard, she told me that she could hear the voices of the dead, though her beloved Cecil's was not among the voices she heard. I feared that this was further evidence of her troubles, but she appeared calm enough, so I brought her home and set to make her some tea.

Since Mr. Ashcroft's death, she has refused to enter the dining room where he was killed. I took the tea to the parlour where she usually took it, but found her sitting on the floor in the spot where the poor man's body had lain. "I've found him, Marie!" she told me. "His last thought was for my safety." And then she said nothing more, dissolving into weeping yet again.

I thought this to be nothing more than an extension of her hysteria, but then something most odd happened later that afternoon. Mistress Eleanor takes an afternoon rest after tea, and when she retired to her chamber, I could swear — and please don't think me mad — I saw her pass THROUGH the door to her chamber without opening it.

I fear there may be forces at work beyond my understanding, Doctor, and I wonder if you might think it wise to have a priest come and bless the house?

I eagerly await your advice.

Yours most sincerely, Marie"

"I'm not sure what to make of that," Eliza said when Esme finished reading. "It might be a trick of her imagination after being cooped up with a woman who was desperately mentally ill for years."

"You might be right," Esme agreed. "Do you think we've learned all we can, then?"

"For now. Let's call Father Whittaker and have him come round to get us. We can go look at the Rosetta Stone while we wait." She slipped the Veil fragment back into her shirt pocket. They said their farewells with thanks to Randall and Tiberius, then climbed the two flights of stairs back toward the ground floor. When they exited the stairwell, the store clerk was waiting for them and slipped them back out through the shop. As they stepped back into the entry hall of the Museum, Esme's hand reached out and grabbed Eliza's wrist. The younger woman trembled and her eyes were unfocused. "He's watching," she hissed, then shivered and stumbled, the trance broken.

"Who's watching?" Eliza asked, snaking her arm around her sister's waist to support her wobbly frame.

"What?"

"You said someone was watching, Ez."

"Did I? Must have been the whispers. I wonder who?"

Eliza sighed in exasperation. Esme's episodes were impossible to make sense of sometimes. "Come on, Ez. Let's get you outside. Maybe that'll refresh you a little."

Esme didn't resist as Eliza guided her toward the staircase that led back down into the courtyard in front of the Museum. The rain had stopped, and people had gathered around the café, eager for a hot cuppa. That seemed like a good idea, even if they had to stand because the chairs were all wet.

Eliza went and procured two cups of tea and returned to find Esme looking around frantically. "What, Ez? What's wrong?"

"He's here! They told me he's here!"

"He who?" She didn't need to ask *who* told Esme. Her younger sister had been hearing voices for years, though they usually whispered to her while she was painting.

"I don't know. But *he* does. He knows who we are. He knew we'd be here. He wants the Veil, Liza. He wants to take it from you." Esme's fear was palpable.

"Where is he, Ez? Did they tell you?"

"He's inside. He's watching."

"It will be okay, Esme," she reassured her. "We're in public. We'll just wait for Father Whittaker here where all these people are."

"It won't matter, Liza. He knows how to get things. He *knows*. We have to go. We can't put Father Whittaker in danger."

Eliza's brain spun, and part of her was grateful for something she could analyze. "All right, listen. We're going to walk over to that low wall like we're going to sit and drink our tea. Then we're going to make a run for the gate. It's not too far to Tottenham Court Road station. Can you run that far?"

"I ... I think so."

"You have your Oyster card?" Eliza asked, referring to Britain's all-access transport pass.

Esme nodded.

"Okay. Wait for my signal, then *run*."

Esme nodded again, grateful that her sister never doubted her, even if Eliza couldn't understand Esme's gifts or how they worked.

They walked toward the wall Eliza had indicated, a long stone structure that functioned more as a bench than as a divider between the concrete and the grass. Esme looked surreptitiously over her shoulder and noticed a tall figure facing them, standing just behind one of the towering columns at the entrance. "Liza, I see him! He's wearing a blue overcoat."

"Okay, then, ready ... steady ... NOW!"

Esme hated to turn her back on the tall figure, but there was no way to both run and watch at the same time. They dashed out the gate onto Great Russell Street, tossing their untasted tea into a trash bin that stood by a nearby food truck. They ran for a couple of blocks, then cut down Bloomsbury Street toward the Tube station. As they rounded the corner, Esme hazarded another glance and caught a flash of blue as the man gave chase.

The Tube station came into sight, and the women ducked inside, gasping for breath and digging for their cards. There was a backup at the turnstiles, and Eliza thought her heart might leap right out of her chest. After what seemed like minutes (but was probably only a few seconds), she and Esme slapped their codes over the scanner and dashed through the metal gates toward the south platform.

It was crowded at this time of day, and they hoped that they could lose themselves in the crowd. They moved to the farthest end of the platform, closest to where the back of the train would stop.

They'd been lucky. The train was only two minutes away according to the lightboard that hung from the ceiling. They positioned themselves behind a group of noisy American tourists and watched to see if the mysterious figure emerged from the station. They had just started to feel the wind in the tunnel from the approaching train when the blue overcoat appeared. The man had a driver's cap pulled low, and tinted glasses obscured his features. But he was definitely scanning the platform, searching.

"Stay lower," Esme hissed. "I'm taller. I'll watch him."

"Bully of a time to rub that in," Eliza grumbled as the train whizzed into the station.

"MIND THE GAP," announced the voice on the PA system. "MIND THE GAP."

When the train doors opened, the sisters kept the tourists between them and the platform. Esme kept watch as the man in the overcoat walked toward the front of the platform and studied the occupants of each car. Esme's breath quickened, hoping they had enough time to escape. She shoved Eliza lower, so that she was literally squatting beside one of the handrails. Esme herself bent her knees so that she'd be less visible behind the Americans who were challenging each other to "Tube surf" by balancing without the help of the handrails when the train moved. The blue overcoat was nearly at the end of the platform when the doors began to close.

Both girls let out a *whoosh* of breath as the train began to move. Esme stood to her full height and tried to get a good look at the face of their pursuer.

Esme's eyes locked on the man in blue. Her mouth fell open. Eliza's iron grip on her arm revealed she had seen the same thing ... a ghost.

6

THE MIRROR AND THE MOURNER

Eliza studied the notes she'd taken in the Archives long after Esme had gone to bed. The world outside the Canterbury Lodge Inn grew still as the shade of night lowered over the city. They hadn't been allowed to take any copies from the Archives, but with her near eidetic memory, the copy of the poem they'd been given was still at the forefront of her mind. The resemblance between the phrases and the traditional Twelve Days of Christmas were uncanny, though the tune didn't work.

Faraday sat with his back to her, gazing at birds out the window, cackling at them when one got too close for his liking. *One stands alone.* Surely the poem had nothing to do with the cat.

Find the tree whose fruit bears seeds in threes. That could mean anything. *The tree* could be her father. He stood tall and proud, unwavering in any storm. *The fruit?* Could that be the Wren children? But how could a poem from centuries ago know about the descendants of Christopher Wren? He was a bird, not a tree. Eliza decided you could make any of the lines mean anything you wanted it to, if you just read into it right. It reminded her of the Quatrains of Nostradamus.

The ninth wears crimson beneath white, the line echoed the metaphorical style of Nostradamus. *The great man will be struck down in the day by a thunderbolt.*

This poem was explicitly ordered from one to twelve, each stanza holding a coded clue. Nostradamus used similar esoteric numbered references. *Twenty years of reign, three brothers*, etc. Each implied hidden timing or sequences.

Unlike Nostradamus, this poem had a deliberate progression, with each stanza building upon the last, forming a prophetic arc, suggesting to Eliza that each might refer to a different artifact. *Did each of these clues hold a meaning that might lead them to the Manifest?*

The doves fly not apart, had to be an allusion to the two of them, Esme and Eliza. Their father often referred to them as his turtle doves. *But only the true heir can hear them?* In olden times, girls could not be heirs to a father's estate. That could only mean Elias. Right? But her brother was missing, presumed dead.

Esme had insisted the man that had followed them onto the Tube had been her brother. Her *dead* brother. Eliza's brain said she'd seen her brother, but maybe it was her heart. She wanted very much for him to be alive. However, she'd spent the last ten years trying to convince her heart he was dead, hoping that her brain would follow.

There was enough circumstantial evidence to convince the scientist that Elias was dead. He'd vanished during a mission, but there was no blood — no body. That might have been sufficient evidence to cast doubt in her mind, but if Elias was alive, why hadn't he come home?

Absence + time + silence = death

It was a tidy theory, mathematical, logical. Even the brilliant Elias Wren couldn't refute her math. While he was brilliant, he was reckless. Yes, brilliant, but he made enemies. He should have known better.

Frustration was easier to bear than her grief. Admitting she still held hoped to find him was dangerous. It would reopen a wound she'd managed to stitch closed with iron threads. Had she known about Elias's mission, or her brother's involvement in efforts to take down the Covenant, she might have gone after him, had she the courage and impertinence of her sister.

Yes. Esme would have gone after him. Eliza was more reserved. She'd have begun a hunt for the paper trail. No one could just disappear anymore. The internet, interconnected banking systems, passports, and other tracking methods would make it too hard for him to just go silent and not resurface somewhere. She had access to the systems that would allow for the search without any of the questions, had she only known to look.

No. Her mind told her to move on, but the nightmares never got the memo. She'd never cleaned out his room, not that his mother would allow it. She still had his number programmed into her cell phone. She never changed it. Sometimes she called just to hear his voice on his voice mail message. She took out her phone as she curled up on the bed, too tired to read any more. She dialed her brother's number and flinched when it beeped loudly.

"Hey, this is Elias. I'm probably in a lab, a library, or jetting off to some far warmer climes. Leave a message — unless this is Esme. You already know. Check your sketchpad, dove. I'm on it!" He laughed, and the tears flowed from Eliza's eyes unchecked. "Seriously, leave a message. I'll call you back. Promise." *Beep.*

Eliza hit the button to disconnect before it had a chance to record her sobs. She'd wanted to tell him to call her. To come home, but she didn't have the strength left today. But she knew better. He wouldn't have let them wonder this long. He loved Esme too much for that. If even Aegis couldn't find a whisper, then the trail must have been cold. It was better for her to think he was gone. Grief was easier than false hope.

Eliza tucked her phone under her pillow. She was drained and spent. Less than three hours of sleep the night before had barely carried her through the day. Exhaustion overcame her grief, covering her like a thick blanket, enveloping her, holding her as she slipped into the darkness of a troubled mind, and broken heart.

Eliza stood alone in a corridor of endless arches: white stone, impossibly tall, like the bones of some ancient leviathan. Each step echoed twice. The floor beneath her was a mirror, but her own reflection did not match her movements. It moved a beat faster than she did, blinked when she did not. Above, the bells tolled in an asynchronous rhythm, their tones discordant and disturbing.

At the far end of the corridor stood a figure shrouded in black — tall, feminine, featureless beneath the black lace that floated around her as if underwater. The woman raised one gloved hand, beckoning.

Eliza tried to speak, but no sound came. Her voice was ash in her throat.

As she moved toward the woman, the arches wept black water. It dripped from above in slow motion, each drop a bell toll, staining the mirrored floor with inkblots that spread into skeletal shapes and keys. She slipped down, fell into the mirror itself and found herself beneath the corridor.

Upside down.

In the world beneath, the arches were ruined. Burned. The shrouded figure no longer beckoned, but screamed, soundlessly, her hands clawing at the black crêpe.

Eliza looked down at her own hands and found the Veil wound tightly around her wrist, cutting into her skin like barbed wire. She tried to pull it off, but it only grew tighter, wrapping up her arms across her chest, entwining itself around her throat.

A ghostly shadow hovered over her as dots danced in her eyes. "Elias?"

The apparition didn't move. She fell to her knees, eyes wide. "Elias? Is that..."

But the mirror above her shattered, raining down glass. Like razors, it cut her flesh and blood merged with the tears that escaped her eyes. "Elias! Help me!" she gasped.

The ghost lifted a finger to his lips, a silent signal not to speak the unspeakable. Then came a whisper — not from the ghost, but from Eliza's own lips.

"The nest is bleeding ... and we're already too late."

She jolted awake, gasping, sweat-soaked, the pressure of the Veil still phantom-wrapped around her neck.

Eliza sat upright in bed, breath ragged, the sheets tangled around her limbs like bindings. The room was cold, too cold. Her skin prickled as if the screaming woman in her dreams still grasped at her throat. Across the room, the long velvet curtains stirred, revealing the gray light of the pre-dawn hours. Then she felt it — the soft thud of a paw on the coverlet. Faraday.

He padded up beside her, silver-taupe fur the same color as the morning light. He didn't meow or purr, just looked at her. Eyes wide, gold, and unblinking.

A knowing look.

Too knowing.

He pressed his head against her shoulder, then curled into her as she rolled onto her side, as if to anchor her and to say, *you are safe here.*

Eliza placed a trembling hand on his back. "It was only a dream," she whispered, though the words didn't taste true. Faraday rolled over, tucking his head beneath her chin. He stayed, warm and quiet, until her pulse slowed and the shadows softened. And in the far off depths of the unfamiliar suite, something creaked. A door. A floorboard, or perhaps a memory stirring in the dark.

A knock, soft and hesitant, came at the adjoining door.

"Eliza?" Esme's voice was muffled, the consonants caught in the old wood. "Are you awake?"

Faraday's ears perked, but he didn't move from his post beside his mistress. Faraday had always been Eliza's cat, though the family might have thought otherwise. Eliza swung her legs over the side of the bed, the dream still clinging to her skin like the morning chill. "Come in," she said, her voice hoarse.

The door creaked open, revealing Esme in an oversized cardigan, her hair a wild tumble of curls. In her hands, she held her sketchpad. "I ... I couldn't sleep either," she said quietly.

"What did you draw?" Eliza knew her sister like she knew her own mind. If she was up in the pre-dawn hours, there was a reason for it. She often channeled her own nightmares into her sketchbook.

"I don't know why I drew this," Esme said, hesitating, but finally came over to the bed and climbed in beside her sister.

Eliza's gaze dropped to the page. Her stomach lurched.

There it was. The cathedral, jagged and towering, distorted by charcoal strokes like smoke — like fire. The mirrored reflection, a beat ahead. A tree with no roots. The black veil draped over a faceless figure. The arching columns and behind one, a shadowed figure, barely there. Watching. Waiting.

"That's Elias," Eliza said before she realized the words were forming.

Esme blinked. "I didn't — it's not like I meant to draw him, I just ..." She looked down at the page, her finger brushing along the shadowed face. "It felt like something falling into place on its own."

Eliza took the sketch book from her gently, her fingers lingering on the edge of the paper. The dream was still raw in her memory — but seeing it rendered so clearly in Esme's hand made it real. Too real.

"The Veil..." Eliza murmured. "It's showing us something."

Faraday stood then, tail flicking, and padded to the window. He sat with his back to them, eyes fixed on something in the darkness beyond the glass.

Esme moved to Eliza's side. "You dreamed it?"

Eliza nodded. "Every detail." She moved her finger over the screaming woman, then the arches, and the mirrored floor that cracked and shattered.

For a moment, neither spoke.

"Do you think he's trying to tell us something? Elias?"

Eliza's jaw tensed. "If that's our brother, that's his ghost," she said, pointing to the ghost. "He's dead."

But the words cracked at the edges and Esme didn't argue.

Outside, the cathedral bells of Canterbury began to chime the hour.

Three.

The witching hour.

And within the soft ring of it, Eliza thought she heard something else beneath the sound.

Breathing.

Not hers. Not Esme's. Not even Faraday's.

No. This was something deeper.

Waiting.

7

TWIN VISIONS

E sme poked at what was left of her salmon as she and Eliza sat in silence on the lodge's restaurant terrace. They had spent the entire day in the lodge under surveillance, just in case the Covenant had found a way to track them. The hours had ticked by without incident, and an uneasy quiet had befallen the sisters since their Tube encounter compounded by Eliza's nightmares.

"Eliza," Esme began, "I know you don't want to talk about it, but we both saw —"

"We both saw a man in an overcoat, tinted glasses, and a hat. That's what we saw, Esme."

"If that's all you saw, why did you grab my arm?" She'd been dancing around it all day, but Esme was determined to see the conversation through this time.

"Look, Ez, I know we both had the same thought. And the guy we saw was roughly Elias's build. But it wasn't Elias. Solan mentioned him the night before, and we were both thinking of him, perhaps because of all this Covenant business. Elias is *dead*, Esme. You've resisted that, I know. But he adored us. If he were alive and out there in the world, don't you think he'd have been in contact? Would he have let us grieve him?"

Esme set her fork down and stared toward the Cathedral Refectory House a few yards away. She wasn't sure what to say. Eliza had a strong, logical point. But Esme couldn't deny the feeling that her brother was out there somewhere.

"Don't be angry with me, Ez. I wish I could believe like you do; it might hurt less. But my mind prefers facts to faith."

"I don't think it would hurt less," Esme answered absently. Her mind was on her lost brother, the way he used to let her win at games (but make it look like he was trying), the wide smile that so few people had ever seen. Esme had kept the stack of his full sudoku puzzle books in the back of her closet for the past decade.

"Come back to me, Esme." Eliza patted her sister's hand. "We have to figure out what to do next. I don't think we should rely on the Order to come up with a plan; we need to think for ourselves."

Esme was still distracted, but trying to focus on Eliza's voice. This was no time to let the whispers carry her away. "What do you think we should do?"

"Let's consider what we know about the Veil and what its powers are. Solan said it might begin to affect my mind since I've touched the bit I have." She tapped her breast pocket, where the coin-like container was tucked away. "I don't particularly want to go mad, so the sooner we wrap this up, the better."

"Do you think it's affecting you?"

Eliza shrugged. "I'm not sure I'd know if it was. My moods are a little off, but that might be on account of ... I don't know ... having had a man die in front of me and subsequently having been chased by the man who quite possibly killed him."

"And then there's your nightmare," Esme pointed out.

"There is that. But again, that could be my mind trying to process the events of the last few days. God, has it only been three days?"

Esme nodded. "The letter we read in the archives made it sound like Eleanor Ashcroft developed some sort of powers. Marie thought she saw her pass right through a door."

"Yes, well, I imagine there was something more to that than what she wrote in the letter, but it does bear some thought. Marie also hinted that perhaps Eleanor was able to commune with her husband when she stood in the room where he died, so there might be something to that as well."

"That doesn't sound very logical of you, Liza," Esme teased. Eliza gave her a sour look, but then smiled, glad that the tension between them was gone.

"I'm beginning to accept that these relics don't always adhere to logic as I understand it," she sighed. "I guess 'there are more things in heaven and earth, Horatio, than are dreamt of in my philosophy.'"

"Paraphrasing *Hamlet*? Mother would be proud."

"It's a nice night. Why don't we walk over to the Cathedral? We can just make the last admission time," Eliza suggested.

"Father Whittaker said to stay here."

"Since when do you follow rules? Besides, there are still lots of people around, and I'm tired of being cooped up. If the Veil *does* have the ability to affect my mental health, I have to do whatever I can to combat its influence, right?"

"I suppose you have a point."

Eliza charged the meal to their rooms, deciding that it was quite fair for the Order to pick up the check, and the sisters walked out of the lodge and down the road toward the main entrance of the massive Gothic structure.

As they passed two black metal posts marking the beginning of the pedestrian-only zone, the world tilted around Esme. She was no longer seeing the outside of the Cathedral and the dusky evening; instead, she found herself walking down a dimly lit stone hallway toward a door that led to someone's private apartments. Her knuckles rapped at the heavy wooden door, but the hand she saw was not her own.

"Enter," came a voice from behind the door.

"I have news, beloved, and I hope you will not be angry with me." The voice coming from Esme's lips was male, husky, and edged with anxiety.

"That depends entirely on your news, Nyx." The woman closed her laptop and fixed her gaze on her visitor.

"I hope you will forgive me for taking some initiative, but I didn't want to mention my hunch to you if it turned out to be nothing."

"I take it, since you are bringing it to my attention now, that it ended up being ... something?" Her eyes shone with intrigue, and she had never looked more beautiful. Whoever this woman was, the man loved her.

"Something indeed. Since we knew the Wren sisters had a piece of the Veil, I took it upon myself to stake out St. Paul's. I figured they'd have to take it to the Order, and that they probably wouldn't waste time in doing so."

The woman leaned forward, but did not interrupt.

"It took less time than I even expected."

"And ...?" The woman was practically vibrating with excitement.

"I was hoping to catch them on the way in and get the fragment from them, but unfortunately, I wasn't able to intercept them. I waited, and when they left, I followed them. I hadn't accounted for the younger one's intuition, though, and she sensed my presence. They made a run for the Tube, and I gave chase, but I wasn't able to stop them from boarding the train and getting away."

"So far, I'm leaning toward being angry with you, Nyx." Her features darkened into a scowl. "I hope you have something good to wrap this tale up into a pretty bow."

"My plan didn't go off as I'd hoped, I admit, but here's the most surprising part: I don't believe the Order took the Veil piece from them."

"So they still have it? The Order didn't put it into any kind of containment?"

"No, they had too much of an aura of magic around them when they left St. Paul's. Only a relic gives off that kind of energy. Which means ..."

"... that the Order intends to try to use the fragment to track and take the Veil!" she finished.

"You know that I live to serve you, my Queen. Let me recover the missing piece of the Veil and deliver it to you myself instead of leaving such a crucial task in the hands of some Warden."

"You would risk exposure to the Veil to serve me?" Her smile broadened into something almost predatory.

"I would risk anything to serve you. You know this."

"It is settled, then. The Wrens are not Agents, but you would do well not to underestimate them again."

"I won't. I'll be better prepared next time we cross paths."

"You have never failed me, dearest, and your loyalty shall be rewarded. Now close the door and ..."

"Esme!" Eliza was shaking her, and the older sister's eyes were anxious.

The world came back into focus, and Esme found herself reaching for the knob on a bright blue door near Christchurch Gate. Was this someone's home? She didn't know.

"How did I get here?"

"You've been babbling for the last five minutes. It's like you were sleepwalking, but I couldn't wake you!"

"I ... what was I saying?" The images which had appeared so vivid a moment ago were beginning to fade.

"You were saying that you wanted to try to get the Veil. You were talking to someone."

Though hazy, the waking dream came slightly back into focus, and Esme quickly told Eliza everything she could remember before it slipped away again. Eliza wouldn't forget.

Eliza looked around nervously, then put her finger to her lips and led her sister to the Cathedral. It was 4:02, but the docent smiled kindly and let them in anyway, reminding them that the site closed at 5.

Once inside, Eliza pulled Esme toward a stand of votives meant for visitors to remember those who had passed on, or to offer prayers for loved ones who suffered.

"So this person in your dream ... he was the man who followed us?"

Esme looked up at the beautifully arched ceiling, the grey-white limestone glowing in the day's fading light. "What makes buttresses fly, Eliza?"

"Esme! Back to Earth! Was it him?"

Esme focused her eyes on her sister. "Yes, I'm sure of it. And he means to take that piece from you, Eliza. But there's something ... off. Something that doesn't fit."

"What, Ez?"

"He lied to her. He said he followed us from St. Paul's. He never mentioned the Museum. Why would he do that?"

Eliza's jaw dropped open. "I ... I don't know."

"But that's important, right?"

Eliza nodded, thinking. She began to walk along the left aisle of the sanctuary, and Esme trailed along behind her. Tourists milled about, stopping to take pictures of the architecture and stained-glass windows, but

Eliza dodged them, her mind whirling with the new information Esme had offered.

Ahead of her, a clutch of people were taking photos of an unusual sculpture mounted high on the wall which looked like a pair of jagged swords. A dull thrum of electrical current pulsed in her pocket, and without thinking, she reached in and retrieved the Veil fragment.

Below the swords, a scene came to life, and Eliza stood transfixed. It was like watching a hologram, but somehow she knew that no one could see the images but her, not even Esme. A man clung to a spectral stone column, a priest ... his hands shackled, and his face a portrait of terror. Four armored men surrounded him, and as the poor man protested, one raised his sword and brought it down on the priest's head, slicing through the crown. Eliza gasped, but was unable to look away. The other men in armor attacked, and the cacophony of their brutality turned Eliza's stomach.

Then, as quickly as the scene appeared, it was gone, replaced by an empty space in front of a prayer bench.

"Is it gone, Eliza?" Esme whispered. "You had a vision! What did you see?"

Leave it to Esme to perceive a supernatural vision as a commonplace event. "I think I just witnessed a spectral replay of Thomas Becket's murder," Eliza muttered back. "I see now why his political murder in 1170 inspired thousands of pilgrims to come here over the centuries. But more importantly, I learned something about the Veil. And I have an idea."

8

FACTS TO FAITH

T he Bentley hummed like a caged lion beneath Eliza's steady hands as it devoured the miles northward. It hadn't escaped her notice that Newcastle was 333 miles from Canterbury. Repeating numbers stuck in her craw and she tended to obsess over them. A less scientific mind might point out that repeating numbers were signs from the angels that protected them or that 333 was a sign that the Universe was trying to communicate with you.

In mathematics, 333 was an odd composite number. It was composed of two distinct prime numbers multiplied together. It had a total of six divisors. It was a palindromic number. She could see various mathematical formulae in the back of her mind's eye.

3.33×10^2.

$(3^2 \times 37)$

101001101_2

Headlights cut through the mist coiling low across the empty motorway, glaring off rain-slick asphalt. The windshield wipers clicked in rhythm — methodical, hypnotic.

Inside the car, warmth pressed against the windows, and the dashboard lights cast her sister's face in a soft amber glow. Eliza sat upright, eyes sharp behind the wheel, jaw set in that familiar line of concentration that surfaced whenever she was focused, or frightened, though she would never admit to the latter. It was the numbers that held her focus and kept the real worries at bay. She gripped the steering wheel so tightly her knuckles ached and her fingers grew numb. The road ahead was nothing compared to the storm brewing in her thoughts: the veil, the dream, Esme's sketches, the poem ... *Elias*.

Esme sat in the passenger seat to her left, wrapped in a battered wool coat, sketchpad resting on her knees, the ghosts of graphite smudges on her cheek. She was unusually quiet. Her eyes kept drifting to the roadside hedges, as if expecting something — or someone — to step out of the mist.

Faraday dozed in the backseat, curled like a guardian shadow, his tail flicking now again. Over the heater's hum she could hear the infrequent purr from the tabby's chest, and she found it comforting. Beside the cat, Father Whittaker snored softly, snorting from time to time. The patient priest had been assigned as their liaison to the Order and would ensure they had whatever they needed to accomplish their mission. Solan assured them the priest was up for whatever fate might await them, but Eliza wasn't so sure. He had the air of a more studious sort, rather than one equipped for spycraft. Eliza was convinced they would need the latter.

"I keep thinking the road's about to vanish," Esme said, tapping her pencil to her lips. "But I think we're driving toward the place where it might start."

Ashcroft House loomed in the distance — still hours away, nestled in the cold heart of northern England. Whatever secrets it held, Eliza was certain this journey would change them. There would be no turning back.

Eliza didn't answer her sister. She kept her eyes on the road, her breath fogging faintly in the cold air leaking around the old seals of the Bentley's windows. Esme watched her carefully, twirling the pencil between her fingers like a nervous charm. Eliza could feel her sister's eyes on her.

"I think there's something waiting for us there."

Eliza frowned, her gaze flicking to the rearview mirror, then the empty road. "At Ashcroft?"

Esme nodded, curling her legs tighter beneath her. "It's in my dreams. Not a place. A presence. Like something old finally opening its eyes."

The sound of the windshield wipers seemed louder after that, slicing through the silence with mechanical indifference.

Eliza didn't dismiss her sister — not outright. She'd learned not to. Esme's instincts, strange as they were, had saved them before. But Eliza's rational mind pressed for answers. "Can you draw it?"

"I tried." Esme flipped her sketchbook around and held it up between them.

Eliza dared a quick glance. The page was smudged and rough, drawn in half-sleep. A structure — maybe Ashcroft — but distorted. The angles were wrong. Shadows pooled unnaturally beneath tall windows. Something — someone — stood in a long hallway just out of reach of the light. The figure had no face. Around its feet,were the outlines of birds — whether dead or sleeping, it was hard to say.

"I don't know what it means, but I don't think it likes us."

Eliza's knuckles whitened on the steering wheel. "Then we'll make sure it has a reason."

She pressed the accelerator just a little harder. Faraday stirred in the back seat with a soft, displeased chirp.

The motorway narrowed as they passed into the Northumberland countryside, trees crowding the edges like silent watchers. Esme tucked the sketchpad back into her bag and leaned her head against the window watching as the night blurred.

"Promise me you won't go off alone when we get there," Esme said, eyes closed.

Eliza hesitated.

"I mean it," Esme, added. "Whatever that thing is — I think it's waiting for you."

And somewhere far ahead, the lights of Ashcroft House blinked on in the fog.

It was 3:33 a.m. when Eliza pulled the Bentley into the carpark outside Ashcroft House. Whatever Eliza had been expecting, this wasn't it. She had this stately country manor in her mind, and this was a city cottage if there ever was one. Cottage wasn't even the right term. It was part of a row of houses built in the late 1800s, sandy bricks aged with mildew and soot from decades of traffic.

Father Whittaker stirred and sat up, rubbing his eyes. "We can't possibly be there already," he said. "I didn't even wake up when you stopped for petrol?"

"I didn't stop," Eliza said. "The tank is probably on vapors, but time was of the essence."

"Well then," Thomas said, "we'll worry about that when the sun comes up. I'm sure you're ready for a nap."

Eliza couldn't deny her exhaustion. She'd been afraid of nodding off, especially after Esme did. Faraday had come up and taken his place in her lap as she drove to keep her company. That might have been the only thing that prevented fatigue from sending the Bentley into the gorse and hawthorns of the woodlands or moors.

"Esme." Eliza nudged her sister. Esme flinched and sat up, gasping. Eliza allowed her eye to follow her sister's gaze and realized there was a shadow in the doorway. Her own heart skipped a beat until she realized it wasn't a ghost. The woman was flesh and blood, standing in her dressing gown, her hair in curlers with a net over it.

Eliza collected Faraday and got their bags out of the boot, handing Father Whittaker his bag. "Eliza, allow me to introduce Lady Eugenia Moncrieff, caretaker of Ashcroft House. Eugenia, the ladies Wren. Eliza. Esme." He made introductions as she ushered them into the house clucking like a mother hen.

"Come in, come in. 'Tis as black as the Earl of Hell's waistcoat out there," she said, taking their bags. "And who is this?" She stopped when she found Faraday in Eliza's arms. "What a bonnie wee chitty." She scratched the cat's ears and set the bags aside. "Come. I've kept the kettle on. And a fine idea, if I say so myself. Ye're a bit peely wally." She put a cool hand on Eliza's cheek. "I wasn't expecting you 'til the *porritch* was a-bubblin'." Her Scottish brogue was difficult to translate, but in Eliza's weary brain, she didn't try. She accepted the cup of tea when it was handed to her and all but collapsed into the chair at the kitchen table.

Esme wasn't much better off. She'd been sound asleep upon arrival and it was only by sheer reflex that she reached for the sugar bowl and all but tipped it over her cup. Eliza caught the sugar bowl, much to Esme's chagrin, and added a spoonful to her own cup. Father Whittaker regaled Eugenia with a recap of their journey as he added cream to his own cup. There were biscuits on the saucer in the middle of the table, and Eliza snatched one, setting it on her saucer as she lifted the cup with an unsteady hand. She inhaled the perfume.

Oolong. Wonderful!

"The Ashcroft House was the last abode of Cecil and Eleanor Ashcroft, two of Aegis's finest operatives. God rest their souls," Eliza came out of her reverie to one of Lady Moncrieff's stories. "Poor dear, Eleanor."

"Why do you say that?" Eliza asked, unsure if she was referring to Eleanor's insanity or her loneliness.

"Eight years she lived without her beloved Cecil. Eight years she mourned. I came tae the manse tae find the mirrors draped in black and dark bunting over the windows. Stories say, she kept a candle lit at all hours in the window facing the kirkyard in hopes his ghost might find his way home."

"I hope she rests beside him," Esme said, wearily.

"Ack, auld ghosts dinnae rest when the souls they loved are lost, ye ken. They wander the moors, whisperin' the names o' the lost, waitin' for the wind tae carry them hoom."

Eliza's brow cocked, her nerves suddenly cracking with an ill ease she couldn't define.

"Mistress Wren, I understand you're Beatrice's oldest?" The Lady changed the subject. "You're the ilk of her if I ever saw."

"It's Dr. Wren, actually," Esme said, before Eliza could correct her.

"Eliza is fine," she said, forcing a smile, pushing her glasses up her nose. "I had an older brother, but ... I'm the oldest now."

Eugenia recognized the remorse in her tone. "Ack, forgive me. I had forgotten about your brother. My deepest sympathies." There was a long silence surrounded by slurping of tea and munching of biscuits. Esme yawned, triggering Eliza's own yawn.

"Lady Moncrieff," Father Whittaker said. "It's been a long day and I'm sure the girls are worn to the bone. Do you have a room ready for them?"

"Aye," she said. "Forgive me, lasses. Ma heid's mince. I do. There's fresh linens on the bed, and everything you might need for a bath after sunrise."

"Thank you for your hospitality, Lady Moncrieff." Eliza tipped back the cup and drained it. Esme did the same.

Eliza was grateful to find they'd been put in a room together. The massive four-poster bed was carved from ancient oak and was stained almost black. Its surface was polished by time, but the intricate thistle and stag motifs appeared to be hand-carved. She'd seen a bed like this once in Edinburgh when she'd gone for a summer intersession course at the college there. Thick velvet drapes — deep burgundy, edged with gold fringe — hung from the canopy and were heavy enough to block out the world around them. A fire in the stone hearth had been banked, its coals providing sufficient heat to fight back a chill as they quickly changed into their bedclothes and climbed in under the covers. Faraday joined them, disappearing beneath the blankets, brushing against Eliza's ankle as he curled up around her feet.

Sleep came slow and strange as Eliza lay tangled in the heavy warmth of the great bed, the velvet curtains half-drawn. Faraday purred, tucked against her.

Eliza found herself creeping up the stairs to the loft storage area above the bedroom — a place she'd never dared enter while awake. The air was thick, draped in the scent of damp lace and dried roses. In the dream, it was winter, twilight. Dust floated like ash through the stillness.

In the far corner, she saw the figure, draped in black lace, her head bowed, a candle in one hand, the glint of black glass beads of her rosary in the other. Black as a raven's wing, the Mourning Veil moved ever-so-slightly, though there was no breeze. Eliza couldn't see the face behind it, but she felt the woman's eyes — sunken, searching, sorrowful. A cry escaped her ghostly form like a banshee on the moors.

She tried to turn away, but Eliza's body refused to cooperate. The Veil rose and drifted forward, relentlessly. A sound filled the room. It was not footsteps but the sound of taffeta and silk sliding over the hardwood floors.

"You have what once was mine," the voice seemed to say. "There is sanctity in tears. When someone you love becomes a memory, that memory is a treasure. You must protect my treasure."

"I'm trying," Eliza said. "My sister and I are trying."

"There is no pain so great as the remembrance of joy in the presence of grief."

"I know you miss your husband. I am deeply sorry for your loss." She studied the floating apparition, realizing there were no footsteps as it moved in a circle around her. The hems of her black skirt were ashen and she could make out the trail disturbed in the dust that had accumulated on the floor.

"The Manifest is your destiny, but my Veil is your challenge," Lady Ashcroft said, her voice echoing through time. "But the Veil alone lacks the power you need. Still, you must see it restored before the Covenant learns my secret."

"But I don't know how." Eliza never felt more helpless in her life.

The spirit reached for a broach pinned to the collar of her mourning gown. The black stone glowed with an unnatural light. Her ghostly hand held it out for Eliza to inspect. "He lies beneath the Yew, the root coiled 'round the serpent's eye. Where his body and blood fed the soil, the truth was buried." Eleanor placed the brooch in Eliza's outstretched hand. She was surprised when the jet stone disintegrated and the spectre disappeared with it.

A scream erupted from the bed beside her, and Eliza woke with a sudden start. The cat leapt from the bed and disappeared behind the wardrobe. Esme grasped her sister, shaking her. "I told you not to go without me! I told you!"

"I know how we're going to get the Veil back."

"He lies beneath the Yew, the root coiled 'round the serpent's eye. Where his blood fed the soil, the truth was buried." Eliza repeated the ghostly message over a bowl of oatmeal.

Lady Eugenia Moncrieff pondered this factoid for a moment, then rose and disappeared into the sitting room, returning a moment later with a small leather bound book. It looked as old as the house, if not older. The pages were yellowed and the text irregularly printed, as was so common in the early ages of the printing press. In gold leaf, the title shone in the morning sunlight. *The Language of Loss.*

"The yew tree — a common marker of old graveyards and a known symbol of death and protection," she read. "Cecil's grave lies at the base of an ancient yew on the edge of the kirkyard, nearly swallowed by brambles."

"He's buried nearby?" Esme asked, reaching for another slice of toasted bread, slathering it with marmalade. She'd woken ravenous, unlike her sister, who had not been able to go back to sleep after the nightmare and Esme's response to it.

"Aye, nae sae far from here." Eugenia said.

Eliza sipped her tea, wishing she had something for her throbbing head — perhaps something that would make her sleep. "You don't suppose Cecil had an artifact on his person he was trying to keep from falling into the hands of the Covenant, do you?" She posed the question to Father Whittaker.

"If he didn't, perhaps Eleanor did. Lady Ashcroft was present when her husband died, you see," Father Whittaker added.

Eliza rolled the Lady's message around in her head. She knew the brooch had something to do with it. "She told me the Veil alone lacked the power we needed. I think she tried to give me her brooch."

The sun was lost behind the clouds as they stood at the edge of the old ruins of the medieval cathedral on the outskirts of town. The graveyard dated back to the 14th century, and the stones told tales only ghosts read these days. Along the back stone fence, a lone yew stood like an umbrella blown inside out by a March gale. Its branches reached for the edges of the graveyard, hovering aloft, lower limbs barely above the marble tributes of those who lay in the shade of its branches.

The seed and every part of the tree except the seedcap was poisonous to humans and to cattle, though not to deer or rabbits. The arils, like bright red berries, clung from its branches, falling by the wayside, scattering on the ground like rose petals before the bride on her wedding day. Eliza could picture her father in his garden, trimming his yew trees into elegantly crafted topiaries, creating arches over the stone pathway to the back patio. No one had been so kind to this grandfather tree.

"Here they are, Eliza," Esme got to the stone before she could. "Cecil and Eleanor Ashcroft." Both names had been carved into the stone.

"Okay, it has to be somewhere," Eliza said, scanning the ground around his gravestone, hoping to find a void where the brooch might have been concealed. Eugenia had brought along her metal detector, and scanned the ground beneath the tree.

Eliza worked on a more methodical grid search pattern, working out from the stone. She worked North to South, then East to West, but found nothing to offer any hope. The metal detector had no more luck than she did. She moved to the tree trunk to get out of the wind that rose across the clearing behind the kirkyard. Still bleary-eyed, she leaned against the trunk of the yew, even as the day tilted sideways. The world around her grew silent. And then, came the voice. Soft. Measured. Almost tender.

"The roots remember."

Eliza stumbled and toppled over, landing face first near a void in the tree's trunk. A glint of light drew her and her hand reached for it without her command. The dark stone was cold against her flesh, the pin pricked her thumb as she clutched it. Blood welled from the injury. The voices came on the wind, and Eliza couldn't stop the spiralling of her mind as they chanted an ancient poem in unison.

O Veil o'black, sae fine, sae fell
Ye hid the tears nae tongue could tell
Wi' threads o' hair and widow's breath
Ye've stitched the bound twixt life an' death.
Come hame, come hame, frae ash an' stone
Return to blood, tae flesh an' bone
Where the Aegis lays, sae cold sae deep
Her secrets still in silence keep.
O Mourner's Veil, sae dark, sae wise
Come round ma shoulders, and close m' eyes
And shield me frae the watcher's face
'Til truth walks back tae its rightful place.
O Veil that parts the breathless shore,
Let soul slip through the silent door—
But ken this truth, sae cruel, sae tight:
The brooch alone returns the light.

He parked outside the Greenwich Observatory. If Eliza had any control over her fate, this was where she would come. It was one of the many places they'd visited as children, and he couldn't help but remember the joy on her face upon first stepping foot inside. This was another work of Sir Christopher Wren, who loved science as much as the beauty of a well-crafted building. The observatory was one of his finest works, and many discoveries of the age known as the Scientific Revolution had been made here.

He was weary, but resolute in his mission. He needed more evidence. He had nowhere left to look, and the day was already half gone. He could not go back to the Seer without the fragment of the Veil. He knew she was counting on him. It wasn't fear that stirred him, it was purpose. As he leaned back and tightened his fists around the steering wheel, trying to calm his racing mind, the air shifted and his ears popped. The box in the seat beside him began to tremble and a wailing sob erupted from its depths.

Before he could react, the lid blew off and the Veil rose, reaching towards the north, like a ghostly hand rising from the grave.

"Finally!" Nyx said aloud, relieved that the Veil was finally reacting.

The Veil fluttered in response.

Home.

9

THE TETHER OF THE DEAD

An hour into the journey, Nyx realized where the Veil was leading him: Back to Ashcroft House where its history began. He was astonished he hadn't thought of it himself, but to be fair, the Covenant's documentation on the Veil differed a bit from the Order's. It had been years since he'd seen the Order's files, and there hadn't been a reason for him to pay close attention to it then. He hated to admit it, but he missed the Archives at the British Museum. The Covenant's Hall of Records was extensive, but it was also cramped and dark, and he didn't like sitting there for long if he could help it.

He had read the account of how Thomas Swann had tried to retrieve the Manifest from Cecil Ashcroft, and according to the Order's records, there had been "a struggle" when Swann had tried to take it — a struggle that resulted in Cecil Ashcroft's death. Eleanor Ashcroft's grief over her husband's murder had imparted magical properties onto the Veil that blanketed her sorrow for the remainder of her days. The Order's records warned that contact with the Veil could impart that maddening pain onto whoever was unlucky enough to possess it, and the danger — as far as the

Order knew — was that the Veil could be used by an adept practitioner to control the emotions, and perhaps even the thoughts, of anyone the practitioner wished to influence.

But the Order's records were incomplete. The Veil was so much more than they had deduced. He had forced himself to spend an hour in the Hall of Records before leaving on his mission. The Wren sisters had no idea what they had gotten involved in with this relic, or why the Covenant was willing to kill Niall Roth to get it. He reflected on the conversation he'd had with Maelis before he'd left.

"I see now why you want the Veil so badly, my Queen."

She nodded, her dark hair disheveled from the heated embraces they'd shared before he departed on his mission. "It is the first step to bring us closer to possessing the Manifest. If we can finally get our hands on that book, it will renew and revitalize our purpose. We won't have to pore through histories and legends trying to discover what artifacts might be out there. We'd have the edge over those Aegis fascists … a list of relics Christopher Wren knew about in his lifetime. We must get the Manifest before they do. If they find the relics on that list before we do, they'll be locked away in one of those infernal vaults, and will be of no use to anyone."

Her face was flushed, not with her passion for him, but with her passion for what she considered her holy mission. No organization should be able to decide what magic should exist in the world, and who should wield it. "You read the witness interviews?" she asked him.

"I did. I am not surprised that Eleanor's caretaker failed to report this information to the Order. Had she done so, they'd have thought her mad as well."

"Ironic, considering their own use of magic, wouldn't you say?"

"Do you think she told our people the truth? She was quite inebriated at the time."

"I think we should err on the side of belief, my Nyx."

"The ability to commune with the departed seems quite believable, but the ability to cross between life and death?"

"The Manifest can cross all boundaries of space, and likely time as well. Is it so hard to believe that a relic that was born from the remnants of power it left behind would have the same properties? With the Veil in my possession, I will be one step closer to being able to track the Manifest, no matter where it hides."

He hadn't known what to say to that, so he'd used his mouth to show her how much he'd miss her while he was gone.

As consciousness crept into the corners of her mind, the first thing Eliza became aware of was the familiar rumble of Faraday's purr engine nestled up against her right hip. This was quickly followed by feelings of warmth and softness as her limbs woke to the goose down duvet that was snuggled around her. She felt safe and cosy, and for a moment she wondered if she could drift back off to sleep just to keep that sensation a little bit longer.

The soft creak of the door, however, heralded that such would not be the case. Through her lashes, Eliza could see Eugenia's concerned face poking around the door, a smile spreading on her genteel features when she spotted Eliza's half-open lids. "Oh, ye're awake. Wonderful. Everyone will be so relieved! I put a water on your bedside. You rouse ye'reself, and I'll go fetch ye're sister."

By the time Esme plopped herself on the edge of the bed beside Eliza, the older sister had chugged the glass of water and displaced Faraday in her attempts to sit up. The cat had been appropriately affronted and had re-settled in the chair by the window.

"Welcome back, Sleeping Beauty," Esme chuckled. "We were almost starting to get worried when you fainted in the kirkyard."

"I do *not* faint," Eliza retorted.

"Yeah, okay. Tell that to Father Whittaker and me, who had to haul your dead weight up the stairs. He thought we'd have to take you to hospital, but when you started muttering poetry with a proper Scottish brogue, he decided you were just possessed, so we could haul you back here. He's a priest, after all."

Eliza raised a brow and studied her sister's face, unsure how much of what she's just said was a joke. "Poetry?"

Esme nodded. "I recorded you on my phone and then transcribed it. All about the Veil, about it coming home."

Something stirred in Eliza's foggy brain. "I remember. It's coming. The Covenant's coming."

"We thought as much. Father Whittaker has had folks here warding the house for the last couple of hours. And Solan is sending Agents."

"They won't get here before he does." Eliza wasn't sure *how* she knew, but she didn't have a doubt that the mystery man would get there before reinforcements did. Her brain began to spin, the last vestiges of sleep slipping away. "Where's the brooch?"

"I have it." Esme produced it from the pouch of her hoodie. "We've been getting acquainted."

"Acquainted?"

"Well, sort of. It doesn't whisper, but it hums. It might talk to you, though." She turned it over. "I did find something interesting."

"What's that?"

"It's not just a brooch. It's sort of a locket. Look here." Esme handed the ornament to Eliza.

There was a faint sizzling sensation as the carved jet touched her skin, like putting one's hand on the side of a microwave. The pin was intricately carved into a shape that somewhat reminded her of a chrysanthemum, with its center delicately inlaid with additional polished jet gems. She turned it over in her palm and found that the pin on the back also served as the latch to a small compartment. Being careful not to prick herself again, she opened the clasp and peered within.

Rather than a photograph, which she might have expected, she found a lock of sandy-colored hair. "It's his," she breathed. "It's Cecil's."

"Are you sure, Liza? We thought that maybe it was their daughter's. She died of scarlet fever when she was five ..."

"No, it's Cecil's," she insisted. There was no doubt in her mind. "And there's more of it."

Esme looked at her sister in confusion.

"'*Wi' threads o' hair and widow's breath / Ye've stitched the bound twixt life an' death.*' There's hair woven into the lace of the Veil."

"I'm not sure, but I think that's gross. It might be romantic, though. I'll have to think about it."

"It's important, Ez. Here, help me get up. I need to talk to Father Whittaker, and we need to call Randall."

"Well, now, I wasn't expecting to see your faces again so soon! What a pleasure!" The Archivist's face filled the video chat screen. He was holding his phone at a low angle, giving his head a rather doughy triangular appearance.

"Thank you for taking a few moments to speak with us, Randall." Eliza felt a growing sense of urgency, and it was all she could do to maintain basic social pleasantries. "I hope you'll forgive me for being abrupt, but I have to ask you an important folklore question." She paced through the house, her phone in hand and Esme and Father Whittaker at her heels.

"My favorite kind," he gushed. "Fire away, Dr. Wren!"

"Isn't there some sort of superstition about locks of hair in Victorian jewelry? I remember my mother had a lock of my great-grandmother's hair that was passed down to her. I was very young, but I remember she told me a story ..."

"Oh, yes, a very popular Victorian custom. People often kept locks of baby hair, but often gave locks of hair to loved ones who were going off to war, or even had elaborate jewelry made incorporating locks of a deceased person's hair as a symbol of mourning. Quite popular indeed. The Archives have several envelopes with ..."

"I'm so sorry to interrupt, but I fear time is not on our side. *Why* did people do that? Hold onto locks of hair, I mean." As she passed through the kitchen, she snagged one of the delicious biscuits Eugenia had laid out on the tea tray.

"Oh, there are a variety of reasons. Some believed it held the essence of the person, and thus kept them close to their distant loved ones. But the most fascinating reason is that in some Christian folklore, it's believed that the body must be reassembled on Judgment Day before one can pass through to Heaven. So each of us must go collect any pieces of ourselves we've left behind. Having a lock of someone's hair ensured that you'd have to reunite with them before passing into the Afterlife. Of course, the Victorians didn't know about cellular shed, or else ..."

"Thank you, Randall, that was exactly what I needed to know. I knew you'd have the answer!"

"Well, thank you for the vote of confidence," he grinned, "but what's this all about? Something connected to the Veil?"

"Actually, yes. We found a brooch which belonged to Eleanor which contained a lock of Cecil's hair. Mourning jewelry, I'm certain. And I believe there may be strands of Cecil's hair in the Veil as well."

"Oh! I see! And you believe the purpose of that is ..."

" ... to bring the Veil and the brooch back together. I think they're linked somehow. Like a lock and key."

"My, my. That *is* an interesting wrinkle. What do you think will happen if they're reunited?"

Her steps led her into the dining room, and as she crossed the spot where Cecil Ashcroft's lifeblood had seeped into the wooden flooring, she shivered. The world tilted slightly and her vision blurred into an image resembling a double-exposure photograph with images taken 120 years apart. "I'm not sure, but if my lock-and-key theory is correct, then bringing them back together will quite literally unlock their combined powers. We'll call you back soon." Her voice trailed off and she managed to disconnect the call and grab Esme's arm to steady herseelf before she swooned again. There was no time for her to lose consciousness now.

It was as though each of her eyes was seeing a different time period. The more modern decor of the dining room that Eugenia had curated over the years was overlaid by the phantasmal image of a table with a white linen cloth. Eliza could see Esme's face, her brow knit with concentration and concern, but she could also see a mustachioed man in a tidy white shirt and dark tie, with a tailored striped vest. A leather watch strap hung from his vest pocket, and he wore a surprised expression as he inspected Eliza through his round spectacles.

"What is —" Father Whittaker began, but Esme shushed him.

"Eliza's not alone," she hissed, and the priest's eyes grew wide.

Do I know you? the spectral Cecil Ashcroft asked Eliza.

"No, but I know you," she answered. "I was hoping I would find you here."

Why would you be looking for me? he asked.

"My name is Eliza Wren. I'm with the Order. I ... I need to know what happened to you."

Cecil appeared confused. *I believe I'm deceased.*

"You are. You were murdered by Thomas Swann."

Recognition touched Cecil's features, and the effect was like an air current rippling through a tendril of smoke. *Ah, yes, so I was. He came for the Manifest.* Suddenly his brows furrowed. *Did he acquire it?*

"He did not, as far as we know. It is believed that the Manifest disappeared before he could take it. Your wife, Eleanor, was witness to this. What do you remember?"

Ah, my dearest Eleanor. How she suffered after I was taken from her. But she had the last laugh, as they say. She came to see me many times. Even death could not keep her from my side.

Something about that seemed important, but Eliza's question still hung in the air. "The Manifest, Mr. Ashcroft. How did you find it?"

I did not. A colleague in Edinburgh did. He had found the book in a library in Edinburgh Castle, and recognized that it was not one of their collection. He suspected it contained important information, but he was unable to break the seal, despite trying for many years. Ashcroft sat himself in a spectral chair. *He sent me a message by post, believing that he was nearing death. He gave it to me for further study, but he never suspected the book's true nature. Only that it was several hundred years old and had what he called 'unique properties.'*

"What happened when Thomas Swann came for the Manifest? Why did you fight?"

I couldn't say. There was something too eager in his face when he arrived, and I told him that I would accompany him to deliver the Manifest to the Grand Aegis. Swann refused my offer, of course, and the more I insisted, the more angry he became. I told him that it was not up for negotiation and reached for the Manifest, intending to pack it in my belongings so that I could see it reached the Order. It was then that he attacked me. I remember nothing more.

Eliza nodded, the pressure of Esme's arms keeping her steady. "One more question, Mr. Ashcroft, and then I must set down the artifacts I hold. I fear that extended communication with you is not safe for me. What did you mean about your wife having the last laugh?"

You are right to be concerned. My world and yours are separate for a reason, though I am pleased to see Wrens still in the Order. Eleanor found a way to walk in my world as you have. There was a cost, though, for her travels.

"That's why she went mad." It wasn't really a question, merely confirmation.

Cecil Ashcroft nodded. *Each time she returned across the veil between our worlds, she left a little of herself behind. But in her grief, she refused to use caution.*

"I'm very sorry. But is she with you now?"

He shook his head. *I have a sense of her from time to time, but I believe she may have lost her way. I wait for her here. In time, she will come.*

"I've seen her in my dreams," Eliza offered.

The plane of dreams lies along the edges of the veil. She is just out of my reach there. If you see her again, tell her I am waiting.

"I will." The brooch fell from Eliza's hand and she wavered as the room spun around her. She closed her eyes and took a deep breath, and when she opened them again, Cecil Ashcroft and the window through time were gone.

10

THE SHATTERED TRUTH

Ashcroft House groaned under the weight of the storm. Rain lashed the ivy-choked windows, and thunder rolled like cannon fire in the distance. In the dark recesses of her room, lit by the golden flicker of the fire burning in the stone hearth and a candle on the table beside her, Eliza traced her fingers along the jagged edges of the brooch. The scrap of the Veil, tucked in the pocket of her shirt, quivered in its case, like the pulse of a racing heart.

Faraday's ears twitched as he lay by the fire, her patient warden. His hackles rose. He hissed, low and sharp, and she felt the pressure in the house shift. The cat bolted, darting from the room, as if sensing a mouse somewhere in the ancient hallways. Eliza sat up abruptly.

The electricity had gone out hours ago, but this feeling had nothing to do with the lack of lighting or the heavy shadows that hung in the corners of the room like ghosts. She could sense the wards over the house signalling distress, forcing her own heart to race out of rhythm.

Eliza rose and moved slowly, her own hair prickling on the back of her neck. She moved to the fireplace and picked up the poker from the bin of tools on the hearth. "Faraday?" She moved to follow the cat. A noise in the kitchen startled her, and her feet conveyed her down the stairs silently. The wool socks silenced her footfalls and only the creak of the third step gave away her presence.

Someone or something moved in the entryway. Eliza froze, glancing up at the portraits of each Grand Aegis from the past 75 years. They seemed to convey their trust in her to protect their secrets. Footsteps skittered below. Eliza moved down to the last step, raising her weapon as she came around the corner.

She froze.

A man stood inside the vestibule, drenched and still, puddles gathering around his feet. Her raised hand sank down as he turned, the flash of lighting reflecting off his face.

Older. Harder. Rain-drenched and ghost-pale.

"Eliza," he said. No apology. No warmth.

She stared like a woman struck dumb.

"You're dead," she breathed. "For ten years, I have mourned you."

He didn't deny it. "I'm not here for you. Just the Veil."

"What the hell happened to you?"

"You wouldn't understand."

"Then make me understand."

A shriek from over her shoulder drew Eliza's attention away from the ghost of her brother. Esme came from the Library, running past her. She threw herself at him. "Elias! I knew you weren't dead! I knew it! Where have you been?" She kissed him repeatedly before he took her by the arms and pushed her away. The two stared each other down.

Eliza startled when Esme reached up and slapped him across the face, hard, with her open palm. "Where have you been?" she demanded. "Why haven't you called? We thought you were dead. Well, Eliza did. How dare you do that to us?"

Elias flinched. The flinch gave him away. He hadn't come here to them. He hadn't wanted to be seen.

"I'm not here for a reunion. I just need the Veil. Give it to me." The demand was directed at Eliza.

"You joined them," Eliza said, her voice a blade. "You're with the Covenant."

"You wouldn't understand." He held out his hand. "Give it to me."

Eliza took a step toward him, leaning on the leading foot. "Over my cold, dead body."

"Look, I don't want to hurt you," he said. "But I will take what I need. I need the Veil."

"You mean the Covenant needs the Veil."

A movement behind Elias caught her attention for a brief second. He must have seen her eye twitch. He turned, his fist coming up in defense of his life as Lady Moncrieff came at him with a cast iron skillet. He dodged the blow, more or less, landing an uppercut on her jaw as the skillet clipped his shoulder. The old girl went down hard as he winced, falling back, hitting Eliza and taking her down with him.

The case holding the Veil flew from her shirt pocket and slid across the marble-tiled entryway. It bounced on the threshold and skittered into the darkness of the sitting room. Eliza knew he'd seen it, and clamored over him to grab it. Esme screeched and seized, her eyes going white as a vision came upon her, rendering her of no assistance. Eliza couldn't worry about that now. Elias grabbed her and pulled her back, pinning her to the floor as he tried to climb over her.

The struggle became a roiling ball of arms and fists, knees and feet kicking for dominance, each trying to find the hidden scrap of Veil in the darkness. As children, they'd wrestled over toys and gotten into scrums playing rugby in the yard of Wren Manor. Elias always bested her in games of strength, and occasionally in a battle of the wits, but this was a fight for much more than childish pride. Eliza put her knee into his groin and got to her feet. She crossed the room, begging the heavens to help her find the Veil before he did.

She was bent over, looking under the credenza by the Queen Anne chair when he tackled her and the wrestling match began again. She hit the ground hard. The force of it echoed in her head like a melon hitting a lamp post. Stars danced in her eyes and the room tilted. She recoiled, holding her head in her hands as she curled into a ball. Elias moved over her. "It didn't have to be like this," he said, holding up the case containing the fragment of the Veil. "You made your choice."

Three women sat at the kitchen table staring into their teacups. All of them suffered throbbing headaches and were overcome by a sense of shock, each for a different reason.

The silence was cavernous. Not even the storm was brave enough to fill it. Father Whittaker didn't even dare to speak. He handed Eliza an ice pack, and put a hand on Esme's shoulder. Faraday hopped up onto the table and came over to sniff Eliza's tea, which had gone cold as she sat with the ice pack against the goose egg on her forehead. The cat dipped a paw in the water and licked it, but seemed less than enthused to find the water contaminated by oolong. Instead, Faraday turned to the plate of biscuits and pawed at one, knocking it off the plate. He licked it and approved of his ill-gotten goods. He picked it up in his mouth and hopped off the table, disappearing into the library with his absconded snack.

"And you're sure it was your brother you saw?" Father Whittaker finally broke the silence.

"I didn't want to believe it," Eliza whispered. "Not really. I thought —
I thought maybe if he was still alive, he'd come back to us."

Esme's scowl deepened. "How can you be so calm? Our brother is alive
... and he's working for the Covenant."

"Do I look calm to you?" Eliza snapped harshly. "I'm frantic! My mind
is bruised but spinning a thousand kilometers an hour. I can't wrap my
brain around all of it. And what's worse? He took the fragment of the Veil.
If he is working for the Covenant, they now have it and there's no telling
what they'll do with it."

"They have the Veil," Eugenia croaked, "but not the brooch."

"He didn't know about the brooch," Eliza said.

Esme's gaze lifted, tear-bright and haunted, still unwilling to put words
what she'd seen in her vision. "But he took the Veil."

"And that means he's further along in the puzzle than we are," Eliza said,
standing. She caught the back of her sister's chair to steady herself, before
turning to pace by the kitchen window.

There was a long pause before Esme whispered, "Do you think he's
gone?" Eliza turned to her. "Really gone? Or ... do you think something
has been done to him? Maybe they put a spell on him. The Covenant is
using him against us. He'd never go with them of his own accord." The
younger girl spiraled into conspiracy theories. "What if ..."

Eliza didn't answer at first. Her eyes locked on the spot in the entryway
where she'd first seen her brother — alive. So alive. So changed. She wanted
to believe he'd been twisted by the Covenant — manipulated, cursed,
something that explained why the boy who had held her hand when she
was afraid of thunderstorms would now steal the one artifact that might
protect them all. Esme had the courage to voice the thoughts running
through Eliza's mind, but speaking them didn't make any of it true.

"He made a choice," Eliza said. "Even if something was done to him, he's doing these things now. Choosing to do them."

Esme was quiet, thoughtful. Then, she muttered, "You remember what Mother always says when we lose something?"

Eliza raised an eyebrow.

"If it's meant to be found, it'll find a way to show you where it's hidden."

Eliza snorted a humorless chuckle. "I doubt that applies to turncoat brothers."

They all turned to silence for a moment, thunder rolling in the distance, like the story had paused to take a breath. Then, Esme leaned forward. "We should leave."

Eliza looked at her.

"He knows where we are now," Esme said. "He might come back. He might send the Covenant to find us."

"To what end?" Eliza said.

"He wouldn't hurt us, but ... the Covenant might. And if they find out about the brooch, we could be in danger. Where do we go? Elias knows all our safe places."

Eliza shook her head. "No. I won't go into hiding. If the Covenant has the Veil, they'll be wanting to use it. We know something they don't. We have the brooch. That gives us the upper hand. We need to know what their game is. I won't be outplayed by my own brother. If he thinks I'll sit back and let him rewrite history in the Covenant's name, then he's forgotten who used to beat him at chess."

"Why did we have to leave Faraday at the Ashcroft house?" Esme pouted as they crossed from the train station to the Museum.

"I told you, where we're going, we can't take him, and he'll be safe there. Eugenia gave him a whole can of sardines this morning, and he's quite happy curled up at her feet by the fire. You know I'm right."

"This is a foolhardy endeavor, Eliza, and you know it."

"This isn't a battle of pride," Eliza contested.

"Damn your pride!" Esme snapped. "You always had to one-up our brother. You've been fighting a battle of the wits with him since you were old enough to hold a pencil."

Eliza stopped and caught her sister by the shirt sleeves. "Look," she snapped. "I don't like this any more than you do, but here we are. He played his hand last night and despite what you saw in your vision, he was challenging me to come after him, I know it. I'm not going to let him find the Manifest, and I'm sure as hell not going to let him get his hands on the brooch. I failed to protect the fragment of the Veil, but I am going to make it right. You can help me or you can go back to Ashcroft House and stay there for all I care. This isn't about Aegis or the Covenant anymore. This is a Wren matter."

Eliza turned and went into the Museum, mindless of Esme who stood in stunned silence in the cold grey morning. She made her way to the gift shop and rang the bell. The same attendant came out of the back room and paused. "How did Grendel's mother like her gift?"

"Not one damned bit."

11

BROKEN BRANCHES

Tiberius rubbed aggressively around Eliza's and Esme's pant legs while the girls brought Randall up-to-speed on the events of the past two days.

"So there's no way I'm risking Elias getting his hands on the brooch," Eliza insisted. "We need to put it in a vault."

"I don't disagree with you," Randall sympathized, "but the Grand Aegis has the final say on what gets that level of security."

"I put in a call to him when we reached the outskirts of London," Father Whittaker chimed in. "He is coming here rather than having all of us show up at St. Paul's. If the Covenant is watching, they'll be watching HQ."

"They're right. Elias didn't tell them about the Archives." Esme was scribbling on the leg of her jeans.

Eliza's emotions swung wildly at the mention of her brother's name. "Don't assume he's actually protecting us or the Order, Esme."

The younger sister shrugged, her eyes still puffy from her own grief over Elias's betrayal. "He lied to that woman about where he found us the first time. I saw it in my vision. I'm just saying it might not be as black-and-white as it seems."

Before Eliza could retort, Solan Virell swept into the reading room of the Archives with Charmaine at his well-polished heels. "I'm so pleased to see you all safe." The concern in his dark eyes was genuine.

"I'll feel a lot safer once this thing is in a containment chamber," Eliza grumbled. "It needs to be secured immediately."

"I certainly understand your concerns." His voice was rich and smooth, like molten chocolate as he slid into a heavy wooden chair. "I do think, though, that we mustn't be hasty. This brooch is a heretofore unknown artifact. We don't know what powers it might have, and it must be studied, especially if it's somehow connected to the Veil."

"Show him the poem, Eliza," Esme encouraged, rubbing Tiberius's ginger ears.

Eliza's jaw set in frustration, but she pulled Esme's transcription of the poem out of her bag and handed it to Solan. Randall edged just close enough to the Grand Aegis so that he could read over the leader's shoulder.

"Master Greaves," Solan began, but then flinched when he realized how close at his back the Archivist had positioned himself, "what do we know about the Veil's powers?"

"We know that Eleanor Ashcroft was able to see her husband, at least within the house. We know that she eventually went mad, though it is unclear whether that was a result of the Veil's power."

"I don't know about madness," Esme interrupted, "but I know Eliza has had nightmares, and she's more emotional than usual." Eliza shot her sister an acidic look, as though she'd shared a great secret. "What? It's true. I'm not saying you're irrational or anything. I'm just saying you're showing your feelings a lot more than you normally would."

Rage bubbled behind Eliza's eyes, but the logical part of her mind whispered that the anger she felt was proof. She took a deep breath and willed her pulse to slow. "I suppose I am. And I can confirm that the Veil gives visions of someone's death if you happen to be at the location. I got quite a show at Canterbury Cathedral."

Randall squeaked, though whether it was out of surprise or excitement was anyone's guess. "The letter in the Veil's file suggests that perhaps Eleanor could pass through walls." He was practically trembling and it reminded Eliza of a child on Christmas morning.

"I certainly haven't been able to do that, as the knock on my noggin would attest."

"Ah, but look here at the poem's last stanza. It implies that the Veil and the brooch have additional properties when combined, does it not?" Solan pointed to the lines in question: *O Veil that parts the breathless shore, / Let soul slip through the silent door— / But ken this truth, sae cruel, sae tight: / The brooch alone returns the light.*

"Cecil did say that Eleanor found a way to visit him on the Other Side." Eliza considered the implications of the poem's riddle.

Solan's eyes widened at this revelation. "While I appreciate your desire to put safety first, the need to learn more about the brooch's individual — and perhaps combined — properties outweighs any immediate threat."

"Easy for you to say." Eliza's temper rose again. "You're not the one in danger. You're not the one having nightmares. You're not the one who's been betrayed by your dead brother!"

"He wasn't dead," Esme muttered absently, and it was all Eliza could do not to throttle her.

"Obviously not, as my head and Eugenia's jaw can testify. I'm about ready to put him back in the ground, though."

"I hate to say it, but I think the Grand Aegis is right, Liza." Esme turned to the other occupants of the conference room. "I had a vision while Elias and Eliza were, um, fighting. I was going to ask Eliza if she wanted some tea, but she wasn't in her room. When I heard the ruckus downstairs, I ran into the front hall to help. I must have crossed over the spot where Cecil was murdered, because suddenly I was *there* and saw the whole thing. It was awful." She paused and shuddered. "Any danger we're in is made worse by the fact that we don't know what the brooch does, if it even does anything by itself. I mean, Elias doesn't even *know* about the brooch, so that means the Covenant might not either. It was buried in a tree, after all. There's no reason for him to come after us again right now."

"Just so," Solan agreed, "and in this, we have an advantage. If these two relics are, in fact, bound together in some way, it may even be possible that the brooch could help us find the Veil. We must act *now*, before the Covenant has a chance to learn how the Veil might be utilized. For all we know, they may be able to use it to summon the Ashcrofts' spirits and force information out of them. We must be tactical here, Dr. Wren. Surely you understand."

Against her better judgement, Eliza found herself two hours later sitting in a very plain room in a very plain building in the middle of West Sussex. From the outside, it looked like a boarded up grocer, but inside it was perhaps the most heavily warded room in the south of England. A small council of skilled Agents had gathered to help test the brooch and offer observations.

Drywall columns had been erected in a circle at the edges of the room, each wrapped in iron bands with suppressive glyphs etched into the metal. Candlelight flickered low and blue within the mounted sconces, casting watery shadows across the rune-laced floor. At the center, a pedestal of limestone waited.

Eliza stood beside the pedestal and held the brooch carefully in her hands, reluctant to set it down. The jet stones drank in the light rather than reflecting it. Solan placed himself opposite her, his deep grey ceremonial robes embroidered with the symbols of his office. His eyes wore a calm expression, yet glimmered in the light ... not from nerves, but from the faintest trace of his Seer's Sight reflecting just below the surface.

"Are you sure this is wise?" Eliza asked, for maybe the fifth time. "If the brooch can detect the Veil, if it is a beacon, won't it reach out to Elias —"

"Let it call." Solan's voice was confident. "You said he does not know about the brooch, so he likely won't understand any sensation he might perceive. Besides, we are shielded from all sight here."

Esme stepped up beside Eliza, her gaze encouraging. Reluctantly, Eliza placed the brooch on the pedestal and stepped back. At once the air shifted. Not a sound exactly, but a pressure — a frequency that resonated with bone and blood.

The glyphs on the columns glowed white and pulsed like a heartbeat. A shimmer bloomed in the air above the brooch. A woman's figure, indistinct at first, formed by strands of shadow and hints of lace. Eleanor Ashcroft. Her face was half-obscured by a spectral mourning veil, her lips moving in silent agony.

Esme clutched Eliza's arm. "Do you see her?"

Eliza nodded. Eleanor's figure was all too familiar to her now.

Eleanor's voice arrived not as sound, but as thought — threaded directly into the tapestry of their minds.

He walks where the sea meets stone.

Where blood once sanctified, the Veil still weeps.

The lock is broken, but the binding remains.

Follow what was buried; you will find what was taken.

"Why do ghosts speak in riddles?" Esme whispered, and Eliza elbowed her in the ribs.

Eleanor's image became a spinning gust of wind, lifting the brooch off the pedestal in its torrent as the gathered spectators watched in fascination. Then suddenly, the whirlwind and Eleanor were gone.

The brooch clattered onto the pedestal, landing face down and popping open the hidden locket within. The lock of Cecil's brittle hair glowed red in the silvery-blue light of the chamber, coiling and glowing like a living thing.

Solan stepped forward, his voice hushed. "Cecil Ashcroft ... the hair ... it's responding!"

"We can use it," Esme whispered. "It can lead us to the Veil!"

Eliza stared at the brooch as the hair's glow faded, the brooch inert once more. "Or, lead *Elias* to *us.*"

12

THE LAST PRONOUNCEMENT

Elias paused at the edge of the crumbling Templar's Cathedral and gazed out over the white cliffs, breathing in the damp salt air. The crashing waves of an unsettled sea buffeted against the rocks, the ground reverberating through his thin-soled shoes. The events of the previous night replayed in his weary mind and he couldn't get his sister's voice out of his head.

"What the hell happened to you?"

"You wouldn't understand."

"Then make me understand."

How could he make her understand when he couldn't understand it all himself? He'd woven a merry string of lies over the years, but pushing Esme aside had been the worst thing he'd ever done, that and hitting an old woman and shoving Eliza to the floor. The thud of her head against the hardwood had broken his heart. But he had a job to do.

Once upon a time, he had been considered the future of Aegis. The Golden Boy. Brilliant, daring, charming. He had a gift for ancient languages, cryptic symbols, mathematical equations beyond the ken of even

Einstein. He could unlock patterns in prophecies that even Aegis' most brilliant minds overlooked. They'd trained him in academia and field work, but also in diplomacy and leadership.

The expectations became too heavy a burden to carry. Keeping secrets from his sisters had always been the hardest, but it had been something he'd grown accustomed to. Unlike Eliza, who excelled under pressure, he folded. He was told he was destined to rise, and he believed it, until he didn't.

Ten years before, he'd been in Cyprus when he uncovered pages torn from the Grimoire of the Covenant, the blasphemous counter to the Aegis Order's Manifest. He'd been given strict orders to return any cursed or sacred artifact he came across, but no one ever mentioned he shouldn't read it first. Perhaps because the Order had no idea anyone could translate the long-forgotten languages encoded on the vellum pages.

The Grimoire whispered a truth he had never heard, the truth of the Order rewriting history. The truth that some of the artifacts weren't curses, they were seals, that held something far worse at bay. And his own parents — his own lineage for generations — had covered up the truth and considered the Order the only faction worthy of protecting the world from the use of these magical objects. Many had possible uses in healing the sick, rectifying conflict and ending war. While many held dark magic, there was good in most artifacts locked away and awaiting rescue. Except Aegis blocked the path to redemption and so the curses continued. Worst of all, the Manifest held a prophecy tied to his own bloodline.

A prophecy dooming them all if he couldn't find a way to stop it.

He was doing this to protect his sisters. To protect himself. No one else could do it. It had to be him. He went to the Grand Aegis, but his concerns were dismissed as those of a boy who didn't know the full picture. He asked for understanding. He pleaded with the Council. He arrived at

Wren Manor in disarray and confusion, begging his parents for insight, only to have his own father berate him for going to the Grand Aegis. For questioning the very purpose of The Aegis Order itself.

Disillusioned and dismayed, he struck out on his own, convinced they all feared the truth. He would have to show them. But he was intercepted in Venice by Nyxander Ruelle. Nyxander saw Elias for what he was; brilliant, betrayed, and burning with questions no one would answer.

He took the young man under his wing and began training him to take a different path. He introduced his acolyte to Maelis under an assumed name, assuring the brash young man that Elias Wren's name should never be spoken again. But soon after being introduced to the Covenant, he and his mentor were returning from a mission when they were assailed by an Agent of the Order, Ian Swann. Like his great-grandfather, this Agent of Aegis had a taste for spycraft. Unlike his turncoat ancestor, he was loyal to the Order, and a skilled magic wielder.

Nyxander and Swann faced off in a battle for life and death, a volley of magical spells and the clang of cursed weapons that eventually claimed Nyxander Ruell's life, and left Elias gravely wounded. The foot soldiers of the Covenant arrived too late to help his mentor, but Elias escaped with his life. He lay for months in the *Sanctum Tenebris*, a broken man, wounded to the point of near death. When he arose, he took the name Nyxander Ruell for his own, and vowed he would avenge his mentor's death.

It had been his strength and conviction that had won the attention of the High Seer. She recognized his commitment to the truth, and with truth came privilege. He soon found his way into her bed, and earned the title of the High Ritualist. He was now her Second and she relied on him. She had faith in him to deliver on his promises, and now he had.

The Veil all but hummed in the messenger bag that he wore over his shoulder and soon, the fragments would be joined. But first, he needed to see her.

The spiral staircase to the *Sanctum Tenebris* lay hidden beneath the rubble, warded to protect the Covenant and keep all its members safe. Elias turned back and scanned the expanse to make sure he hadn't been followed before he went over to the stone altar of the Templar Cathedral and rested his hand on its surface.

"*Umbrae patefacio,*" he muttered. *Shadows, open.*

The stones disappeared like a cloud on a rising breeze, and he stepped down into the darkness. Torches illuminated without effort as he grew near, and the stones materialized overhead, hiding his entry into the protected fortress.

The scent of lunavelle clung to the warm air. Rivulets of water ran down her damp skin as she emerged from the steaming stone bath, wrapped in robes the color of eclipse. Her long black hair had been pinned up, though tendrils had escaped their bonds and clung to her ivory skin like wet cobras. Shadows danced across the high walls of her private chambers, carved with constellations and runes too ancient for common eyes.

A flicker of candlelight warped in the polished onyx mirror as the door creaked open behind her. "You're late," she said, voice as soft as falling ash.

Nyxander entered in silence. The Veil fragment, encased in plastic, was now clutched in his hand. His footfalls made no sound against the mosaic tiles, though the floor itself trembled faintly beneath his steps.

"I had to be certain I wasn't followed," he said, his voice low, reverent.

"And my commands?"

"When the Vox speaks, I listen. The fragment and the Veil are ours once again."

Maelis turned slowly, her pale eyes catching the candlelight like frost on glass. She stepped toward him, studying the object in his outstretched hand. A hush fell. Even the candle flames stilled. Maelis extended her hand, hovering over the casing. Her hand trembled in anticipation, betraying the magnitude of her desire to own it, to see it restored and to use its power as the Universe intended.

"So much power," she whispered. "And now you ... bring it back to me."

Nyxander's jaw clenched. "To us," he corrected gently.

Her eyes flicked up to meet his. "To us," she said in a smile that didn't quite meet her eyes. "To us." She brushed his hand aside, catching the front of his jacket, pressing her wet body against him, offering her kiss as the reward she must have known he wanted. He tucked the fragment back into his bag and slung off the strap, setting it in a chair where it was safe, before scooping her up.

"The moon will be full tomorrow night," she said, running a finger along the line of his jaw. When the dawn comes, you will meet with the Lexicant and ensure the wards are put into place before the rituals can commence."

"When the Vox speaks, I ..." her lips captured his before he could finish.

Even as her fingers idly coiled in his hair, memories of his sisters drifted through his mind — ghosts of another life. How had it come to this? Maelis had saved him, yes... but his sisters were blood. Flesh... His hand moved along her flank, a quiet gesture more out of habit than desire.

But this wasn't just about her. His service to the Vox extended beyond her touch. He served the Obsidian Covenant, not the woman. His loyalty was sworn, sealed in shadow and silence. He had to remember that.

"How did you come to the Covenant?" Nyx's voice broke the quiet. A question he had never thought to ask her before.

"The Hollow Seer had a vision of me," she replied, her gaze distant. "I was working in an obscure department of Her Majesty's Revenue and Customs. Disillusioned. Forgotten. I know I would never reach my full potential buried in bureaucracy. And then ... I came here. The Covenant offered purpose. I serve something greater now."

"I serve where I am called," Nyx murmured, invoking the words of the Obsidian Oath.

"And you've served well."

Maelis found him in the hour just before sunset. The Ritual of Binding required preparation, and his day had been occupied by ensuring everyone involved had been trained on their role, the spells that needed to be spoken, and cleansing his own body and mind before moonrise. Nyxander's acolyte prepared his robes and he now stood clad in velvet in the richest shades of cobalt, golden wards embroidered in the edges that ran up the front and over the hood, which lay on his shoulders until the ritual began.

The High Seer had been dressed in a ritual gown that exposed much of her ivory skin, covering the parts only Nyxander was allowed to witness. Black gloves covered her hands and ran up her arms almost to her shoulders. Her hair had been plaited into tiny braids that lifted it away from her face, and ran down her back. A diadem of gold and rubies graced her stately head, while her gossamer skirts only hinted at what was beneath.

She asked nothing of him as he moved through the chamber that was cut from stone in a cruciform layout. He disappeared into the reliquaries filled with broken swords, saintly bones, and sacred texts that had been blacked with ash over the decades. He returned with his ritual items and laid them out on the altar that stood on a raised octagonal platform.

The Choir entered the chamber from another arm of the reliquary and came to stand before Maelis, bowing.

The Choir Master pushed back his hood. "High Seer, we have come to confirm your command for the ceremony."

"Do you have some cause to question my judgment?" She snapped back harshly. It was no secret that the High Seer didn't always meet with the Choir's approval and the Choir of seven men, seven women were the only ones who could even begin to question her authority.

"When the Vox speaks, we listen, your Grace," the Master said. "We only wonder if you know what the outcome of this sentence will be."

Nyxander noticed a hint of a smile shadowing her lovely face. "If the Veil can do what the prophecies foretell, you will have a Warden to put to the sword in the morning," Maelis said.

"But, High Seer..." the Master of the Choir started to protest, but Maelis lifted a hand. "If the Warden is to give his life this night, he cannot be executed a second time."

"Then what you do with him when I am done will be for you to decide. You may stay and observe in silence, or you are dismissed. Choose for yourself."

She turned to the altar and picked up a silver bell, striking it with an iron hammer that was barely larger than a jeweler's mallet. The bell's tone disappeared down each arm of the sanctuary and echoed back, arriving in fours at the central chamber. She took a step down. Before the dais, a depression in the shape of a Leviathan Cross was the Circle of Mourning, its points marked with stone basins once filled with water from holy wells. Now it was tainted with shadows.

The Hollowed Seer, carrying the Veil draped over her hands, entered from one arm, while the other members of the Council entered from opposing arms. Each of the remaining council members carried an obsidian candle. They came to the altar one at a time and lit their flames, taking the pillars to points around the chamber, where they were placed into stone niches to provide protection from dark forces during the ceremony.

The hooded High Ritualist's voice rose in the chamber as he sang the ritual incantations to add further protection. Nyxander had a soft but warm tenor to his voice and Maelis's alto blended into his as her response melded into harmony.

The Warden who had failed her was brought into the chamber, hands bound. He was forced to his knees in the Circle of Mourning though he cried out in protest and begged for mercy.

"Hear me, O Veil of Mourning," Nyxander spoke clearly, ignoring the doomed man. "*Tenebrae nos vocant.* By the breath between, the threads unbound ..." The Hollowed Seer offered the Veil to Maelis, who took it and carried it to the altar. She laid it out across the stone, arranging it so the torn corner was exposed. "Torn threads of sorrow, spun 'twixt life and death ..." He took up a silver blade and drew it across his hand. He held it high so that all witnesses would see his blood had been shared as part of the sacred covenant of all members. "Reweave thy whisper into the weave of truth. By hand and heart, by oath unspoken. Let what was torn asunder now be restored." His blood dripped onto the frayed edges of the Veil. He took the scrap from the plastic case and made sure his blood touched the severed threads. "*Venit umra, redintegra filum.*" A piercing cry rose from nowhere and reverberated off the stones in repeating echoes as he brought the edges together. "Come, shadows. Mend these threads."

Maelis placed her hand on the altar. "*Redintegra filum.*" *Mend the thread.*

The cry morphed into a widow's sobs and tears trickled through the lace and down the sides of the altar, collecting in the depressions around the cross. Even as the widow wept and tears dripped from her Veil, the severed threads twisted, grasping towards one another. Maelis gathered the artifact into the cradle of her arms. She turned to the condemned man who struggled and cried out for mercy. He struggled against the crimson cords that held him, and the Ashwalkers who held him fast in place.

"Your failure to the Covenant frayed the tether between what is and what must never be," she said, her voice both a prayer and a death sentence. "But still, the Mourner must taste Death, for this is the consequence of Life."

She held the Veil over the man's head, as one of the Ashwalkers moved behind him, and raised his sword. In the span of a racing heartbeat, she let the Veil fall over the condemned man, and the executioner struck, piercing him through the back, the blade erupting from his chest as the lace blinded his eyes.

"Through the veil and void, cross over," Maelis said.

"Walk where no living soul must tread," the Hollowed Seer added

The Lexicant took the next line. "But know this, the Gate swings one way."

"What passes through is not returned," Nyxander said. "Only remembered."

With a rising wail the Veil enshrouded the man, the runes sewn into its lace throbbed in glowing red symbols that flashed too quickly for Nyxander to translate. The condemned Warden collapsed onto the blade, his hands falling away as he fell limp. His blood melded with the tears in the basins carved into the floor.

The entire structure began to quake. Pillars fell over snuffing their flames, plunging the chamber into near-darkness. The cries of the Veil faded into nothingness but the screams of wraiths echoed as they materialized over the corpse. Even the Ashwalkers backed away, their duty to the Covenant accomplished. The monstrous ghost-like beings that guarded the veil between the living and the dead hesitated.

"This one's life is not yet done," two of the spirits spoke in a unified voice.

"Death comes too soon," the third added. "He is not supposed to cross the veil."

"Return him to me, as is promised in the prophecy, for he has given his life for the cause and no martyr of the Covenant may die a final death," Maelis spoke the words with an air of haughtiness. "But he is condemned for his misdeeds, and our cause is just."

"Once the veil is crossed, it cannot be undone," the third wraith spoke. "He will go to the place where souls cannot rest, but be warned ..."

The twin wraiths spoke the last pronouncement, "They do not forgive, and they do not forget. The undead remember."

Maelis watched as the Wraiths and the corpse of the condemned man faded into the mists of time and place, and the Veil lay in the pool of blood at the center of the cross. Nyxander could sense her confusion, but faced her wrath when she turned to him, anger flaming in her eyes.

"Why didn't he come back?" she demanded. "He was supposed to come back!"

Elias took a step back, equally perplexed. The prophecies said the Veil would bring them a martyr. He was supposed to be their eternal champion but now, Maelis was left without her prize. "I ... I don't know, my Queen. I did as you commanded."

"And yet you failed," she snapped.

13

THE PENDULUM'S PULL

Esme held the brooch over the map that she had spread out on her bed at the Lodge in Canterbury. She had used the pin on the back to attach the pendulum chain she sometimes used for divination, hoping that Eleanor's pin might help them find the Veil.

"We shouldn't be doing this alone," Eliza advised her. "Not now that we know Elias is working with the Covenant." Eliza paced behind her sister, her anxiety and rage wafting off her in waves. "This may not even work. The Covenant will have wards, just like the Order does. Who knows whether the bond between the two objects can circumvent whatever security measures they've taken?"

"That's exactly why we have to do this ourselves. We don't know who we can trust. Solan wanted us to wait for our parents to get home tomorrow night, but what will they say when they find out Elias is alive *and* a traitor? This will work." Esme was certain of it, though she wasn't sure why. She began to hum to herself as she dangled the pendulum, letting her conscious thoughts slip away to make room for whatever insights the spirit of Eleanor Ashcroft wanted to share.

The pendulum didn't move at first.

Then it twitched.

Then again — stronger this time, as though being pulled by an unseen tide.

It began to swing in a tight arc, then circle slowly over the map ... drifting ... guided not by physics, but by something beneath the surface of the physical world. A spectral strand of hair snaked out from the locket chamber and wrapped itself around the chain, creating an eerie reflection as if moonlight glowed from within, augmenting the morning sun that filtered weakly into the room. Then the pendulum settled, trembling, over a single point.

Dover.

The tip of the pendulum rested at a specific spot near the coast, where the famous white cliffs overlooked the English Channel. "Isn't that where the war tunnels are?" Eliza scrutinized the map.

"Eliza, that's where the Veil is. That's where he went."

Elias. Their brother. Their betrayer. The one who had torn the Veil from them, unraveling more than gossamer fabric.

"He won't expect us to come for him there," Eliza mused.

"No," Esme agreed, "because it's suicide."

The pendulum pulsed once, as if in agreement, and a gust of wind whispered through the open window, ruffling the map. Eliza set her hand on the corner of the paper to anchor it, and the sisters began to plan.

Trying to sneak into a tourist site was easy enough, but trying to sneak in just before dark was another matter entirely. Particularly when the main thing they wanted to see was closed for the season. Eliza and Esme strolled along the walking path, thankful that the windy and soggy November weather kept most of the visitors away.

The Fan Bay Deep Shelter was an underground complex that had been built to accommodate soldiers and equipment during the Second World War. It had an extensive network of storage rooms and tunnels, extending as far as 23 metres below the surface. During the warmer months, visitors could don a hard hat with a torch and tour the tunnels, but at this time of the year, there weren't enough tourists to justify keeping it open. Still, the pendulum had pointed here, so here they were.

Eliza wore the brooch pinned to her sweater, and it pulsed like a second heartbeat beneath the heavy coat she'd borrowed from Father Whittaker. He'd been hesitant to let the girls out of his sight, but they had promised him they'd stay away from home or anywhere else Elias might think to look for them.

They had *not* promised not to head directly into the Covenant's home turf.

"So now what?" Esme asked. "We can't get into the tunnels the regular way, and I'm quite sure the Covenant doesn't either."

"I agree, there's got to be another way in. And I don't think you're going to like it."

Esme pulled her beanie down and jammed her hands in her pockets as the wind whipped over them. "How much am I not going to like it?"

"We're going to have to go around. The only possible way to get access to those tunnels is from the beach."

Esme groaned. Walking all the way back to Langdon Beach wasn't the real problem. They could just move the car and park closer. Navigating the zigzag path in this weather and the climbing down the rusty ladder that led to the shore, however, presented a number of issues that were unpleasant at best.

"I'm sorry, Ez. There's nothing for it."

"Let's crack on, then."

The first few sections of the pedestrian trail were easy enough to navigate, but once they reached the gravel section of the path, they had to hold onto each other for balance. By the time they reached the top of the iron ladder, both of their hearts were pounding.

"I guess we should just be grateful the tide is on its way out," Eliza commented, trying to find some sliver of positivity in her darkened mood, "so at least we won't get stuck as long as we aren't here too long."

They walked along the rocky beach, the sea wind whipping around them and dousing them with mist. Seeing no caves or tunnel access, they returned to the ladder and crawled back up, taking shelter in a man-made stone cut-out with several chambers.

"There has to be some way into those tunnels. We just have to find it," Eliza insisted.

"My trainers are ruined," Esme complained, and her sister glared at her non sequitur. "But you're right. If the Covenant can get in, so can we. Maybe the brooch ...?"

Eliza was way ahead of her. She'd already reached into her coat and detached it from her shirt. The jet grew warm in her hand. "How do you do that trance thing?"

"It's usually not something I do on purpose," Esme shrugged. "I would probably close my eyes and talk to it."

"You can't be serious."

"I don't know, Liza. It's all about intent. You want to communicate with the brooch, right? You want it to show you the way? So if you don't want to talk to it, just concentrate on what you want to know."

This kind of mumbo-jumbo was outside her scientist comfort zone, but Esme was right. She'd have to have a little faith in the science she couldn't understand if they were going to make any progress. She closed her eyes, then took a deep breath and rubbed her thumb over the carved flower design.

"Try visualizing," Esme advised. "We saw the ghostly tendrils of hair before. Picture them reaching toward the Veil. Picture it like an anchor rope guiding you, connecting you."

Eliza did as Esme suggested, and it was as though the brooch had been waiting for her direction. It pulled at her, pointing her feet deeper into the side of the cliff. She began walking through the unlit subterranean passage, trusting that her sister wouldn't let her walk off the edge or into a wall. Though her eyes were still closed, she could sense the light brightening as she stepped into another room that must have had access to daylight. A few more steps and she felt the urge to pause. She opened her eyes and found herself facing five vertical wooden planks affixed to the wall. The blockade was heavily laden with the carved names of visitors and a *NO ENTRY* sign.

"This barricade ..." Eliza scrutinized the obstacle before them. "I think there's another tunnel behind it."

She and Esme began exploring the edges of the boards, hoping to find a loose one. No such luck. A curved stone balcony edged with iron bars provided a view of the blustery Channel. Esme and Eliza stood staring at the tumultuous grey water, thinking.

"It led me here. There has to be a way."

"There are no loose boards and no hinges or a door handle, so if it is a door, they don't want it to look like one," Esme pointed out.

"Hinges ... hinges ..." The scientist in her was processing, and she knew she was missing something. "If there aren't hinges on this side, maybe there are hinges on the other side and it opens inwards." She returned to face the wooden boards, scrutinizing the construction. There was a small drainage trench in the floor that ran underneath the door and continued on the other side. She squatted down and extended her fingers through the opening, feeling for ... *a latch*. There it was! She pressed on what felt like a self-locking gate hatch, and with a click, the mechanism released. The wooden door swung a couple of inches inward.

"Yes!" both women cheered in unison.

There were no discernable lights, so Esme pulled out her phone and switched on the torch. "I hope the brooch guides you well," she said, her voice filled with nerves. "We'll never find our way through this since we don't have any idea where we're going."

"Fortune favors the brave," Eliza sighed, and they plunged into the darkness, closing the gate behind them.

The passageway narrowed, and the damp chalk walls closed around them like a clenching jaw.

Esme followed close at Eliza's shoulder, holding her phone aloft as her older sister led with the brooch in one hand and the other trailing along the rough hewn wall. The light cut a narrow path through the dark — just enough to see the crumbling stones underfoot and the dust curling like ghost breath.

Eliza said nothing. She didn't have to — the tension in her silence said it all.

The tunnel sloped downward, gradually but steadily, deeper into the heart of the cliffs. The air was thick with salt and something else — old incense maybe, or the decay of memory.

Eliza stopped moving. The pulsing of the brooch had quickened, mirroring her own heartbeat. It pulled at her bones, a sensation like gravity folding in the wrong direction.

"Left," she whispered. "There's a breach in the wall, I think."

Esme pulled a rubber-banded group of painting tools out of her knapsack and produced a palette knife. She began to scrape away at the wall where Eliza pointed until a narrow seam in the stone became apparent. A little more chipping away revealed stonework and sigils under the plaster that had been designed to look like the natural stone of the tunnel.

"This is Templar stonework," Eliza breathed, running her fingers over the symbols. "There's an archway." She gave a shove to the plaster beneath the arch and it fell inward in a pile of rubble.

"Let me go first." Esme wedged herself into the opening in front of her sister. "Just in case we run into the Covenant, you can get away with the brooch." Eliza wanted to protest, but Esme was already moving down the passageway. In the distance, a sound ... cold, metallic ... the single toll of a bell. Resonant and rich ... not the chiming of time, but a sound that might accompany a ritual.

The Covenant was close.

As they descended, the pull grew stronger, not just leading them to the Veil, but to more danger than they'd ever been in.

Esme was the first to notice the smell of wood burning. She tapped her nose, and Eliza sniffed the air and nodded. Another turn in the pitch of the passageway, and the thinnest outline of light appeared up ahead. Esme extinguished her torch and the sisters crept toward what must be the entrance to the tunnels.

She held up her hand to feel the barrier that separated them from what was likely another stone passageway and touched something very familiar. Canvas.

They were behind a large painting.

They listened intently, trying to determine if it was safe to move the artwork and emerge into whatever space lay beyond. Soft footfalls approached and the girls held their breath until the sound passed by and was lost in the distance.

After waiting a moment to be certain of silence from the other side of the canvas, Esme hazarded to wrap her fingers under the edge and slide the painting to the side. It had been fastened at the top like a barn door, allowing her to slide it open on quiet tracks.

They stepped through into a room bathed in soft violet light and slid the painting back into place.

The bedchamber was enormous, and perhaps the last thing they had imagined encountering. The stone walls were vaguely curved, perhaps following the shape of the cliffs themselves, and were lined with dark velvet curtains embroidered with silver runes. Between the curtains, framed paintings with mystical scenes adorned the walls, and a single, thin window of delicate crimson and violet stained glass cast a pool of light across the center of the floor.

The air was thick with the smell of incense: myrrh, if Esme's nose was right. Dozens of tall, black candles burned silently, and closer inspection revealed them to be battery-powered rather than open flames.

In the center of the room stood a tall four-poster bed carved from bone-pale wood, perhaps ash. The canopy was draped with delicate black tulle, the bedclothes mussed and knotted in pillowy mounds.

To the left, a full-length mirror in an iron frame twisted to look like rose vines hung upon the wall — but the sisters' reflections seemed out of sync, as though ever-so-slightly delayed. At the far end of the chamber stood a writing desk. Eliza slipped over to investigate, finding it covered with a scattered set of tarot-like cards, their corners worn with frequent use. She motioned for Esme to have a look.

"They aren't like any cards I've ever seen," Esme whispered, and reached out to touch them. Eliza caught her hand and shook her head vigorously.

Esme scanned the room before locking eyes with her older sister. "We were out of our minds to come here alone, Liza."

"I was thinking the same thing," came another voice from behind them.

14

THE TIES THAT BIND

Eliza froze, grasping a hand around Esme's arm. "Oh, thank heavens. Finally someone who can tell us how to get out of these tunnels!" The words may have been false, but Eliza's relief was real. Despite her anger at Elias, she wanted nothing more than to go home, have a cuppa and forget about this whole unpleasant affair. The mundane life of a research scientist in a cold white lab was looking better and better every moment.

The dark-haired woman paused, startled as she found intruders in her private chambers. She wore a dress that covered little. Locking eyes with Eliza, she lifted a hand and the canvas sealed itself behind the two girls. Eliza glanced back, but turned, realizing it wasn't going to be that easy.

"Did you think I wouldn't feel it when someone slipped past my walls?" the woman asked, narrowing her eyes.

"Excuse me?" Esme tried to keep the rouse going. "We ... we're lost. We were with our friends and ..."

"Clever girls," she said. "But not clever enough."

"But ..."

"Nyxander," the name was spoken both as command and communion. The man in dark robes stepped into the room and froze, locking eyes with his sisters. Eliza recognized the fear that gripped him. It was written on his face like a curse long buried but suddenly unearthed, raw and undeniable, aching with truth. "Bind them. We have two more subjects to practice our rituals with."

His eyes also conveyed a warning, and Eliza read him like an open book. He moved and came around to face them. Eliza looked past him at the woman, seeing something she hadn't expected. The Veil lay draped over her sleeved arm, lifting towards them. Eliza's eyes darted, meeting the woman's. Then she glanced down, realizing the light from within the brooch rose into a swirl of cyan energy, reaching beyond the confines of the jet stone, stretching toward the Veil. The Veil responded similarly, and the woman saw it. "What's this? The Veil has a mate?" She turned to Nyxander. "You brought me only half the spell. You've been outwitted by mere girls. These fools have gifted me the final piece of the puzzle."

"You shouldn't have come here," Elias said, keeping his tone low. "This is no place for lost children." The last he spoke loud enough for his Mistress to hear. She moved, circling the girls like a predator as their hands were bound by magical forces they could not see.

Eliza's mind raced, trying to make sense of the moment. She eyed the brooch and could sense the powerful woman's mouth watering. She wanted it. She needed it. She knew the powers of the Veil, but did she know the brooch was essential to the Veil's true magic? "Now, dear girl, you've brought us everything we need."

Dammit. I guess she does now.

The *Sanctum Tenebris* pulsed with latent power, as the Veil rested across the altar like a living thing. The air hummed as the Choir and the Council of the Covenant gathered. Nyxander bound his sisters with sigils of silence and obedience. He suspected Esme might have the power to break his spells, but for now, they were on their knees in front of the altar, flanked by Ashwalkers.

Maelis had taken the gem pinned to his sister's shirt, and the Hollowed Seer was busy trying to commune with the Oracle of Ancient Wisdom to ascertain the powers of the relic.

While Maelis was away, it still was not safe to communicate with his sisters. He needed them to understand that if his true identity were revealed, it would mean certain death for him, if not for them all. Eliza seemed to sense it, but he wasn't sure about Esme. His *little dove* rarely showed restraint when it came to him, and had it not been for their encounter in Ashcroft Manor, she might have run to him and thrown her arms around him right there in Maelis's chambers.

As it was, both his sisters cast daggers in his direction whenever they caught sight of him. He had to find a way to convey the need for extreme caution in a room full of the High Council, as well as the Choir.

His mind raced with panic. He needed the Veil to appease Maelis. He needed his sisters safely away from this place. He'd never meant for them to find him. Esme must have used her visions to hone in on him somehow, now that she knew he was alive. Eliza, though. Whatever possessed her to allow Esme to lead them here? That wasn't like her. She was studious to a fault, not prone to leaving the safety of her comfort zone. She would be missing her textbooks and her gizmos. She liked to tinker and make things — mechanical things. Of course, he'd been gone for ten years. They'd both grown. Esme hadn't changed a bit, except for being several inches taller than her older sister. Eliza though, was not the young college girl he remembered. He was sure of it.

"Nyxander," Maelis called him. "Come join us."

The Hollowed Seer's chamber beneath the Templar church flickered with the cold, unnatural light of *spiritflame*. Its blue white glow cast no warmth. It saw only the truth. The Hollowed Seer hovered at the edge of the smaller altar in her Chamber, her eyes clouded with the milky sheen of second sight. Her skin was etched with runes, her voice pinched as her soul spoke the words of the ancient Ritual of Seeing. "*Oculus veritas, lux revelare*," she muttered the incantation over and over, swaying as the words hovered in the cold air. *Eye of truth, reveal the light.*

The old crone's hand hovered just above the artifact, not touching, but feeling all the same.

Nyxander stood beside Maelis, still cloaked in his robe, surrounded by lies he could only hope to keep hidden, if only for his sisters' sake.

Then, the air changed.

"This artifact," whispered the Hollowed Seer, her voice like parchment turning to ash, "does not belong to this world. It was not made by hand, nor by spell. It was given. Or found. It knows the names of the Dead. Those who will rise when the final days arrive." She turned her sightless gaze toward Maelis. "You seek to summon a soul. This brooch does not summon. It binds. It remembers what was loved."

Maelis leaned in, her expression taut with fascination. "Can it bring them back?"

"Not as you would have it done," the old woman cautioned. "Your husband of many decades gone is the one you want, but this artifact can only bind what is already bound. If you wear it, the dead will know you, but I cannot say if he will follow you back."

Nyxander's head whipped around to the old Oracle, brow arching as he realized what Maelis had planned, realizing he'd been played.

Maelis leaned closer. "But it does bring back the dead?"

"The Veil is the door ..." the Oracle said. "The brooch is the key."

"Then I have two souls to test my theory on," Maelis said.

Nyxander stepped between her and the brooch. "You can't."

Maelis's gaze snapped to him. "I must."

"They are not part of this," Nyxander protested.

"On the contrary," she said, lifting the brooch gingerly from the pedestal with her gloved hands. "They are the thread, and I will stitch them into the fold, whether they weep or not."

The Hollowed Seer turned her blind gaze to Nyxander and whispered something only he could hear. "You must choose your tether, son. The living ... or the dead."

Nyxander caught Maelis's arm. "You would really take the lives of two innocents?" She stopped, glaring at his hand on her person. Her brow lifted as if to question his courage — or his foolishness. "They're just girls."

She narrowed her eyes at him, suspicious. "They are mine to do with as I please." She let out an exasperated sigh. "And quite frankly, you have been a disappointment. First you fail me by not discovering this necessary artifact, and then you question my authority to use it. *Veritas ex Tenebris*, my love." She reached up and patted his cheek. "Truth from darkness. It's the motto of the Covenant. *Lux Revelat Occulata*, the motto of my family. Light reveals what is hidden." She clucked her tongue. "While you have been a pleasant distraction, my heart will always belong to Alaric. If the Veil indeed has the power to reunite me with him, I would even sacrifice *your* soul."

The vitriol in her tone told him she meant it, too. He'd heard about Alaric Varrow in stories told around the hearth after dinner on cold winter nights. He was a Covenant Agent of Legend. He'd been the High Ritualist many years before. Nyxander took a step back, considering his position for a moment. He didn't believe she'd really sacrifice him, but he knew Maelis wouldn't hesitate to try it on one or both of his sisters.

"Does this mean you wish me to vacate my post as the High Ritualist?" he spoke with the hesitance of a man rejected.

"When Alaric is revived, you may vacate then."

"When the Vox speaks ... I listen."

He'd listened alright. While he'd been loyal to her, her loyalties lay elsewhere. Elias grew angrier as he returned to the *Sanctum Tenebris*, where his sisters knelt before the altar. His mind raced. He had to get them away from Maelis before she could execute her plan, execute his sisters. a

Maelis lay the Veil on the stone altar, then placed the brooch atop it, the pin nicking her finger as she secured it to the Veil. The chamber grew quiet as she took her place and raised her arms to the Covenant. "Let it be written, the Veil shall fall, the boundary shall bend. Bring her back whole, but unawakened."

She moved around to stand before Esme.

Elias moved to stand beside her, his voice shaking. "Don't do this, Maelis." She met his gaze and fire flickered behind her eyes. "She's my sister."

Maelis turned slowly, studying Esme's frightened face. Eliza scowled, struggling against her binding. Elias began the silent meditation necessary to release his sisters' bindings.

Maelis chuckled darkly, a wry smile curling in her cheeks, one of pure evil. "That explains everything."

"Leave my sisters out of this!"

"But I can't, Nyxander. She is a vessel. You said so yourself."

"That is not the one," the Hollowed Seer spoke.

Maelis moved to gaze into Eliza's eyes, a wicked smile still etched on her face. She slid behind the older sister and did not hesitate. She withdrew a silver dagger from the folds of her skirts and grasped Eliza by her hair, tilting her head back, dragging the blade across her throat. Eliza's gasp was cut short by the sickening snick, precise as parchment sliced with a scalpel. At that instant, Elias's unbinding enchantment activated and the ropes fell from Eliza's and Esme's hands. Panicked, Eliza's hands went to her throat as a haze of red tinged the room. Maelis turned to take up the Veil and brooch, placing them on the sacrifice's head.

"No!" Elias screamed. Eliza coughed, her eyes imploring her brother's for salvation.

"*Umbrae vocem audite ... anima fracta, redi ad nos...*" the Vox chanted, the Choir and the Counsel joining in.

Blood gushed through her fingers and ran down the front of Eliza's sweater. She inhaled, blood filling her lungs, gurgling in her windpipe as she fought against the coming dark. Elias dropped to his knee, his own robes stained with blood as he caught her in his arms. Esme grasped her sister's hand, and the three Wren siblings were soulbound for one fleeting moment.

Eliza's hand fell to the brooch, pressing it to her chest, blood gurgling from her mouth as she gasped for breath. Behind the Veil, her eyes flickered, then went slack. With one last heave, her soul escaped her body and a single tear ran down her cheek.

Esme's eyes rolled back in her head, going white with the shadow of her vision. Elias could feel her being pulled into the void, and he held onto them both — the anchor for them in the world of the living. It didn't stop his grief from escaping his body. "Noooo!!!!"

"She is not alone," Esme whispered in the world of the living. "We are stitched together. Blessed be the ties that bind."

The space was vast and silent, carved from obsidian and shadow, lit only by the gentle glow of starlight spilling through cracks in the firmament above. Eliza stood barefoot on the black stone floor, her clothes torn, her hands stained with her own blood. Around her rose towering pillars etched with hieroglyphs that whispered as they shifted.

In front of her stood a golden scale. Ancient. Celestial. Each pan balanced with impossible precision. On one side, a single white feather, magnificently light, radiated with divine clarity. The Feather of Ma'at. On the other, her heart, still beating, glowing faintly within an impossibly thin vessel of translucent quartz.

From the gloom stepped a figure cloaked in twilight. Esme, or some vision of her, stood in the linen robes of the temple priestess, her eyes rimmed in kohl. Her voice echoed with layers that were not her own. "This is not a dream," she intoned. "But neither is it death. Not yet."

Eliza turned, the weight of everything she'd lost etched across her face. "Is this my judgement?"

Esme nodded.

"Every soul must pass through truth to return. The scales must balance. If the heart is heavier than the Feather of Ma'at, you will be lost."

And then, a voice, deep, sonorous, ancient as the Nile silt, rumbled through the hall. "***Let the weighing begin.**"

The jackal-headed figure of Anubis, emerged from the shadows, his hand steady as he adjusted the scale. Nearby, the Devourer Ammut, stirred. The part-lion, part-crocodile, part hippo paced, its breath hot with hunger.

The feather floated serene.

Eliza's heart pulsed, trembling with doubt and worry, burdened by grief, rage and guilt. Esme reached out and lightly placed a hand on Eliza's shoulder. "Remember who you are. You are not just blood and sorrow. You are so much more."

Then something unseen tugged at Eliza's chest — a glowing tether, silver and scarlet. Elias. In the land of the living he knelt beside her body, his own blood mixing with hers as he drew the blade across his wrist, letting the red rivers run down his arms until they melded with hers. Wren blood was strong blood. The brooch between them pulsed with a shared memory, one of joyful tears. Of happier times. "Come home, Eliza. Follow the threads. I've got you."

The scales shifted. The heart grew lighter, not because her sins vanished, or her anger abated, but because she accepted them for what they were. She'd worn these things like a cloak, and now, she shed it, tossing the mantle of the past away.

Balance was achieved, and Ammut growled with hunger, but accepted the pronouncement. She would not feast tonight. The Devourer roared once and vanished into smoke. The light around the feather flared, then lifted on the air and came to Eliza's hand. It landed lightly in her palm. Esme smiled, her form starting to blur. "It's time."

The Veil lifted, and the brooch burned bright. Eliza gasped, alive again.

15

THE VEIL WITHIN

Darkness. Muffled echoes. Then screaming. A sound like breaking glass had been given a voice.

At first, Eliza thought it was her own voice piercing the air as she returned from Ma'at's judgement. But as she unclosed her eyes, her vision filled with a silhouette in black lace lit by the battery-powered candlelight. *Eleanor.*

Maelis took a step back, startled by the piercing noise and the appearance of the widow's spectre.

You'll not have her while I still walk the threads of the world. It was not a sound, not exactly, more of a thought with ragged edges that reached into the minds of everyone in the chamber.

The Hollowed Seer gave a dry chuckle, like wadding up a sheaf of crumbling parchment. "The Dead have their own agenda, it seems. I warned you that they do not serve the living."

Maelis shot her a venomous look, but then set her eyes on Eliza. "Perhaps, but my experiment was a success nonetheless. Behold," the Covenant's Queen addressed her followers. "this one returns from the

Other Side! She may be wounded, but blood no longer flows from the wound. Have I not promised you that we would conquer Death itself?" There was a soft murmur from the Choir.

Nyxander — no, he was Elias; he was no longer Maelis's pawn — exchanged a look with Esme, whose eyes had lost their ghostly sheen. He transferred Eliza's weight into Esme's arms and raised himself to glare at the woman he had once loved.

As Eliza's body shifted, a gleam of light caught Maelis's eye. There, in Eliza's palm, lay the Feather of Truth. Maelis and the Hollowed Seer gasped in unison as Ma'at's gift radiated an unmistakable aura of divine power.

Eliza struggled to sit, but her limbs wouldn't obey. Then a whispering wind slid through her mind: *Let me in, child, just for a moment. Let me carry you.* The madness was gone from Eleanor's voice, replaced by a quiet strength and resolve. Eliza didn't speak; she didn't have to. She *yielded*, and the silhouetted spirit before her dissipated into a mist.

Eliza's vision clouded, like seeing the world through a smudged pair of glasses, but she rose gracefully to her feet, propelled by Eleanor's will. To Esme, it looked as though Eliza rose on strings of shadow and silver. The older Wren sister's eyes blinked, at first cloudy and unfocused, then sharp and unnatural. She took a tentative step, not with the stagger of the wounded, but with the poise of a queen stepping through fire.

"Liza?" Esme whispered.

Eliza turned. Her lips curved up at the corners. When she spoke, her voice carried an echo.

"She's resting. I'll carry her now." Eleanor, for so it was, pulled the Veil off Eliza's head and held it in her right hand with the brooch, gazing at them as one might an old friend. In her other hand, the Feather shimmered.

Maelis spat, "Your parlour-possession tricks are nothing." She struck like a serpent — silent, sudden, and desperate. As one hand closed around the Feather, the other brushed the Veil. And then the world shattered.

The room froze — fire stilled, sound collapsed into silence. Even breath halted mid-motion.

Maelis was no longer among them.

She stood in a desert of black sand beneath a star-choked sky. The sand shifted, and in front of her rose a platform of obsidian upon which stood Anubis, tall and still as a monument. A scale hovered before him.

The goddess Ma'at stepped in front of the scale, her bronze skin shimmering in the moonlight. A Feather, similar but not precisely the same as the one Eliza had been clutching, floated out of her crown and hovered over one of the scale's plates. The goddess nodded at Anubis and he raised one muscular arm.

Maelis felt it instantly, a tightening in her chest, a sharp, unnatural pull. She gasped. Her limbs were locked, her will stripped away.

"No. No. Wait, "she said, voice cracking. "This is an illusion. I don't belong here. I served." But her words meant nothing. A shadowy image of her heart tore free from her breast, writhing like smoke, and floated obediently to the other side of the scale. The weight settled.

"No," Maelis breathed. Then louder, more shrill: "NO! I guided the faithful! I am the Seer! I am the Vox!"

The black sand roared and split. Ammut emerged, vast and monstrous, crocodilian jaws gaping wide, lion's mane bristling with malice, hippopotamus feet thudding on the platform. Her eyes were endless hunger, her gaze final.

Maelis backed away, stumbling, hands outstretched. "The world needs me! I served! I spoke for the rights of the world! I gave my life to the cause!"

The Feather flashed once.

The scale dropped.

Anubis lowered his arm.

Ammut lunged.

The scream Maelis gave was not human. It scraped the stars and turned them cold. Her soul didn't just fall, it crumpled, shriveled, torn from itself and dragged beneath the sands. A final pleading hand reached skyward, then vanished into silence.

The black sands stilled. Only the gods remained.

Maelis's form collapsed like ash before Eliza's feet. A brittle wind scattered what remained.

Eleanor stepped forward and raised Eliza's left hand. The Feather, now resting in her palm, shone like a torch against the darkness. "Your Queen has been deemed unworthy. Who else," Eleanor said, her voice echoing through the realm, "wishes to have an accounting of their sins?"

There was a collective gasp from the Choir, and even the two Ashwalkers drew back in fear. In a scramble, they fled the chamber, all but the Hollowed Seer, who sat serenely on her stone bench. She cocked her head to one side, perhaps perceiving Eleanor's presence even through her blindness, but she made no move toward them. "Fly away, Wrens," she tutted, "before the serpents return to swallow you whole."

"This way." Elias gestured to the passageway behind them, tucking the Veil and brooch into Eliza's coat pocket. "She's right. They won't be afraid for long. They'll return with weapons."

They made their way through the dim passage, Eleanor's spirit giving Eliza's body the strength to move at a relatively normal pace. Elias's heart pounded. The Covenant guards would certainly catch up with them at this rate.

Somewhere beyond the pain, beyond the torn edges of her body, Eliza floated. Not in warmth or peace, but in *stillness* wrapped around her like silk. She could still feel the magic of the brooch and the Veil woven into the threads that bound her to her body. She was aware of their flight down the darkened tunnel, and of Elias's fear that he could not safely return them to the surface before the guards intercepted them.

Even in this form, her analytical mind reached out, trying to see if she could navigate the tunnels ahead, even if just as reconnaissance. She sensed the presence of *others*, not living people, but other ghosts who walked the tunnels, and in her mind, she beseeched them for help.

"Stop!" Esme hissed. "Elias, wait!"

"We can't stop, Esme. They're undoubtedly following us by now." He tugged at her arm.

"The child is right. We must pause. There are those who would assist us." Eleanor echoed through Eliza's mouth.

The air shimmered ahead of them, and the apparitions of two Knights Templar in chainmail draped in gossamer tabards emblazoned with what were once red crosses appeared and wavered in the darkness. They gestured toward an arched alcove which had been framed with curtains and decorated with a tall, standing candelabra.

"They're showing us a way out," Esme surmised.

"Esme, they're *dead*." Elias hesitated. Then, as an afterthought to the knights: "No offense, chaps."

"So was she," Esme gestured at Eliza.

"And still I endure," Eleanor replied. "And if your sister is right, then Cecil ... my heart, my home ... is waiting for me just beyond the veil."

Elias sighed in resignation and began probing the alcove with his fingers. One of the knights passed through the curtain just to the right of the hidden entrance. Esme pulled the heavy fabric back to reveal a crumbled section of brickwork. It wouldn't be easy, but with a little effort, they'd be able to maneuver themselves through the hole. She began to wiggle her way through, widening the hole as she went by pushing any loose bricks through the hole ahead of her.

Once he realized what she was doing, Elias ushered Eliza through and then, with some difficulty, followed. He took a moment to arrange the curtain as well as he could to hide their escape before following his sisters down the tunnel the phantasmal knights had revealed.

After what seemed like an eternity of navigating in the darkness, they emerged from beneath a tangled blanket of ivy near one of the massive concrete WWII structures known as the Fan Bay Sound Mirrors. The sound of the incoming tide roared below in the darkness.

"Our car is that way," Esme pointed. "Maybe a kilometre."

"No, I'm sorry, Dove. I can't go with you," Elias sighed, drawing his sisters into his arms. "I'm a man without a country, as it were. If I see you again, it will be because the world is ending — or I am."

16

The Valley of the Shadow of Death

E sme didn't remember much about the escape from the tunnels, nor the hike back to the car. Had Eleanor not been there to help support her sister, she might not have made it.

She certainly didn't remember anything about the drive to King's College Regional Medical Center in Canterbury. It was the top-rated trauma center in the region, according to a quick internet search. Esme only remained aware of the endless pressure of her blood-slick hands on the steering wheel, and her own thundering heart hammering against her breastbone.

Eleanor stayed with her for as long as she could, assuring Esme her sister's heart continued to beat, but the younger sister knew the injury had done significant if not irreparable damage. *If* Eliza survived, the damage might even be permanent.

Somewhere along the journey, Eleanor parted in silence, leaving the sisters to their fate.

Eliza remained pale, her lips almost blue as she slumped in the passenger seat, her breath shallow. The bleeding had stopped, though the amount of blood on their clothing was the stuff of horror novels. The real concern was the rattling rales in her chest as Eliza tried to draw breath. There was no time to tarry. Esme drove at a breakneck speed in the pre-dawn hours before the morning commuters roused from their beds.

At the hospital, Esme skidded into the ED lot, and flew from the car, bursting through the doors, screaming "She needs help! My sister!" Her voice cracked like glass, drawing every eye. Esme could no longer hold her fear or emotions at bay. "She's been attacked!"

The receiving nurse started shouting, calling for a doctor, a gurney, and a crash cart. She followed Esme into the car park, rushing to open the car door. Her eyes flicked to Eliza's pale face, noting the darkening blood on her skin and clothing and the gaping wound across her neck. Eliza, slumped to the side, appeared lifeless. The nurse reached to take a pulse, but thought better of it. "She's alive?"

"Barely. Please! Help her," Esme begged, tears cutting tracks down her wind-pinked cheeks. "Someone slit her throat. We were hiking when we were mugged in the woods. We got separated ... I heard her scream ... it all happened so fast..."

A doctor shoved Esme aside, moving past the nurse to get to his patient. He hesitated, and Esme could see a look that told her he was certain it was too late. "Does she have a pulse?"

The nurse had Eliza's wrist in her hand. "It's very faint."

"Get that gurney in here!" the doctor shouted.

Esme was jostled aside as the team swept Eliza on to a gurney and through the double doors. Someone tried to guide Esme to a chair, but she resisted, craning her neck to get a glimpse of her sister as they rushed past her into one of the trauma bays. Esme stood in the door, numb, her heart hammering in her chest, as if hers could beat hard enough to keep them both alive.

"Wait!" Esme raised her hand. "She's — she's allergic to penicillin!"

A nurse came over and drew her back into the hallway. "Any other allergies or health conditions?"

"No," Esme stammered. "Not that I know of."

"Previous surgeries?" the nurse jotted down notes.

"Knee surgery," Esme said. "When she was 14. She tore her ACL — right knee — playing cricket with our brother."

The nurse scribbled it all down. "What's her name?"

"Eliza," Esme suddenly felt faint.

"Eliza what?"

"Wren, Eliza Wren. Dr. Eliza Wren."

"She's a doctor?"

"PhD," Esme said. "She's a polymath. Her brilliant brain might be the only thing to survive the apocalypse." She wasn't sure where the words came from, but they spilled out of her unchecked. If Eliza's body could survive this assault, her brain might certainly outlive the cockroaches.

"And what's your name, dear?"

"Esme," she stumbled back. The nurse caught her arm and led her over to a chair, sitting down with her. "Esme Wren."

"Esme, is there someone we can call for you? Your parents, perhaps?"

"They're in Spain. I'm expecting them back any time."

"An uncle then, an aunt?"

"Father Whittaker, maybe," she thought aloud.

"Yes, a priest would be good," the nurse said.

"Does she *need* a priest?" The look of horror on her face must have startled the nurse, who surely hadn't intended to frighten the girl. It was too soon to know if Last Rites would be needed. Esme didn't know if it might already be too late, after all, Eliza had been dead once today already.

"No, no, Heavens, no. I just meant you might need someone to comfort you. We've got your sister. Dr. Trentadue is one of the best trauma surgeons in the UK. You're lucky he's on duty today. Give me Father Whittaker's number. I'll call him for you."

Esme fumbled in her pocket for her phone and handed it to the woman, too numb to even pull up the number. She glanced down at her light gray sweater and cringed at the darkened blood that soaked through the layers of her clothing.

"I'll get you something clean to wear," she said. "Wait here, and I'll go make that phone call."

Dr. Leo Trentadue conducted the primary survey of his patient in under 30 seconds. The ABCDE's — airway, breathing, circulation, disability, exposure. The gash in her throat was clean, precise, but exceptionally deep. The trachea and jugular had been sliced through. Despite the location of the wound, the patient had maintained a functional airway, though only God knew how.

He could hear fluid in her lungs when he listened with a stethoscope, though there were no signs of tracheal deviation or subcutaneous emphysema, which was unexplainable. "Let's get her on O_2 via a non-rebreather mask," he ordered. "Type and crossmatch, start warm saline, stat."

"Yes, doctor," the nurse attending him went to work. Other members of the trauma response team also jumped into action, anticipating the doctor's needs.

Dr. Trentadue focused on the wound. It tracked along the platysma, deep enough to touch the sternocleidomastoid, but not sever it. "Let's get a CT angiogram and a chest X-ray. Call ENT for a consultation. I've never seen anything like this. Do we know what happened?"

"Her sister said someone cut her throat, but I don't have any other details."

"Have the police been called?"

"That's the first call I made," one of the assisting nurses said.

"This girl should be coding on my table. What's her BP?"

"She's tachy at 78/42," one of the staff said.

"Open the IV and give me another check," he ordered. "I want a trauma panel and let's get an OR ready."

Dr. Jasmine Patel arrived a moment later, peeking over the medical staff as they worked on the patient and she sterilized her hands with hand sanitizer, then reached for a pair of gloves. "What do you have here?" she saw the blood, then saw the gaping wound.

Dr. Trentedue briefed his colleague on his patient's condition. "She should be dead."

"How did you get the bleeding to stop?"

"I didn't," he said. "She was like that on arrival."

"No clot should hold like that," Dr. Patel moved in to examine the wound. "Let's get her up to surgery. We need to assess the vascular issues before she strokes out."

The fluorescent lights above hummed, casting a sterile glow over the quiet expanse of the recovery room. Machines beeped in a steady rhythm, measuring her oxygen levels and every beat of her heart. Eliza lay motionless in the bed, her neck swathed in clean white gauze. A clean hospital gown lay over her chest. Electrodes, wires, and tubes ran from her body to the machines. Her mussy braid lay heavily on her shoulder. An oxygen cannula rested under her nose and the sterile perfume of clean air provided comfort.

The nurses assigned to the ward stood on the other side of the glass partition. "I've never seen anything like it," the OR nurse said to the ICU care nurse. "She came in with massive trauma to the neck — her throat cut ear to ear — clean through the trachea and jugular — but when Dr. Patel got her to the OR, the worst of the injury had healed."

"Healed?"

"Scar tissue had already formed and looked as if it had been there for weeks. It's impossible. All they had to do was close the skin." A murmur of awe passed between them as they moved away, voices fading.

Esme came around the corner and stopped, her eyes following the nurses as they went about their business. She turned, and found the room number on the doorway. They'd been talking about Eliza. She stepped into the room and moved to the side of the bed, standing still like a sentinel for a long moment, her fingers lightly brushing Eliza's hand. Her own eyes were rimmed red, but dry now. She had wept herself empty. Father Whittaker came and stood behind her, a comforting presence with his hands folded, his head bowed in prayer.

"She shouldn't be here," Esme whispered to herself. "But she is."

Eliza took a deep breath, letting it out in a long faint sigh as her lids fluttered, still heavy from the medication, not fully free from the sedatives. The monitors continued their calm, metronic hum. Outside, a cardinal chirped against the gray skies over Canterbury. Inside, in the small room filled with machines and miracles, Eliza Wren began to wake — not quite whole, but very much alive.

Her lips parted, dry and silent, her throat instinctively trying to form sound — but only a rasp escaped. She winced, her hand lifting weakly toward her neck, but not quite making it. Esme caught it and held it between her own trembling hands.

"Don't try to speak yet, love," Father Whittaker said gently, stepping to the other side of the bed. "They say it might take some time. The trauma was ... considerable."

Eliza locked eyes with Esme. Esme's voice trembled as she leaned closer. "You came back."

Eliza blinked slowly, lifting a shaky hand, her finger curling open to point as Esme, as if to say, *you brought me back.*

"Elias brought you back, too." Esme's voice cracked at the thought of their brother. "Maybe we haven't lost him completely."

Father Whittaker placed a hand on Eliza's shoulder. "Esme told me about your journey across the veil and back," he said. "While only God may judge, He may come in many forms as only He sees fit, and I praise Him for your return. We had faith in you — in both of you — all along."

The door snicked shut behind them as Esme and Father Whittaker stepped into the hallway. The corridor was quiet, save for the distant murmur of hospital life — a cart rolling past, a monitor chirping, soft footfalls on linoleum.

Esme leaned against the wall, arms crossed over her chest. She stared straight ahead, her voice soft but not urgent. "She's not the same, Father." It wasn't a question.

"No," he said simply. "She won't be."

Esme swallowed hard, as if the cut had breached her own throat. "It was the Veil. The Brooch. But it wasn't just magic. I saw where she went. I felt it. I followed her into the land of the Dead." Her voice broke at the truth, tears flooding her face.

"You aren't the same either, my dear," he put an arm around her. "Neither of you will ever be the same again. But she passed the test of judgment, and she's back. You need to focus on that."

Esme shook her head. "She didn't have to plead her case. The threads between us ... they were weighed too. Her soul isn't hers alone any more.

It's ours ... and not just hers and me. Elias' too. He's bound to us. I don't know what price he paid, but he was the one who brought us back."

The priest's jaw tightened, a flicker of concern etched across his usually serene features. "There are ancient laws, Esme. Older than magic. Older than Aegis or the Covenant. A soul returned may carry something with it. Not everything that crosses the veil between this world and the next can come back clean."

Esme nodded. "I suspected that might be the case."

"Eliza is no different," he said. "Whatever followed her back, she can't outrun it."

"Then I will walk with her," Esme said, her lips curling into the shadow of a smile.

"You always have," Father Whittaker leaned down and kissed her forehead. He lifted a finger as if about to expound something sacred. "*Where you go, I will go ... and where you stay, I will stay,*" he murmured, quoting from memory. "Your bond has carried you through the Valley of the Shadow of Death, Esme. And not even that could part you."

"Is that from the Bible?"

"Ruth, Chapter 1, verse 16-17," he said.

Esme glanced over her shoulder and gazed at her sister laying in her bed of pain. She had died with secrets on her lips, but she woke with something older than memory stirring in her bones. And though she could not speak it aloud, they all knew — nothing would ever be the same again. *Ever.*

EPILOGUE

ALL THAT REMAINS

The hospital solarium smelled faintly of antiseptic and rosemary. Outside the serenity garden lay in hushed decay ... rose bushes stripped to thorns, ivy blackened with frost.

Eliza was wrapped in an oversized chenille cardigan, pale but conscious. An IV stand and stats monitor blinked lazily at her side, and Esme's fingers were entwined with her sister's on the arm of the wheelchair.

Simon and Beatrice Wren stood near the windows, the grey light blurring the lines on their faces.

Simon hadn't spoken for nearly five minutes. He kept staring out at the dying garden as if hoping it would provide him with answers to the myriad questions washing over him. "He's alive," he said finally. "Our son — alive. And you're telling us he was working with people who very nearly got you killed."

Eliza winced — not from pain, but from memory.

Esme answered for her. "Yes, but he helped us escape. He turned on them in the end." It was a weak consolation in some ways. The Covenant hadn't *almost* cost Eliza her life. Their High Seer had, in fact, killed Eliza as a sacrifice. If not for the artifacts, Esme would essentially be an only child.

Simon turned to face her, his expression unreadable. "Turned on them. Not because it was right, not out of love, but because he'd been betrayed."

Esme met her father's gaze without flinching. "Because he regretted what he'd done. Because he loves us. That counts for something."

Beatrice sank into the chair opposite Eliza, her hands trembling. "You say it was Elias, but was it? Are you sure? It wasn't some glamour ..."

Eliza pulled her hand free from Esme's and began typing on her phone's note-taking app. *It was Elias. But he's not the Elias you remember. He's still our brother, but the Covenant broke parts of him.*

Beatrice's eyes welled up, but no tears fell. "Then we haven't lost him. Not completely. Not yet."

Simon exhaled through his nose. He looked older. Hollowed out.

"I buried my son in my heart years ago. And now I have to imagine him walking around with blood on his hands and magic in his head."

"He's alone now," Esme pressed. "He can't go back to the Covenant, and he can't come home to the Order."

"And if he reaches out?" Beatrice asked.

Then we'll be ready, Eliza typed.

Outside, a crow landed on the stone wall near the window. It blinked once, then flew away as footsteps approached from the hallway.

Simon sat next to Esme and patted her knee. "Then we wait," he said. "We heal. And we wait."

The footsteps stopped at the doorway to the solarium, and Solan Virell's outline filled the frame. "I apologize if I'm intruding..." he began.

"Not at all, Grand Aegis," Beatrice sighed wearily. "You are always welcome."

He approached with the confidence and certainty of a man who knew the power of his own presence. He wore a dark coat, impeccably tailored, with a small silver glyph of the Order embroidered on the collar. His dark eyes landed first on Eliza, then swept to Esme and their parents.

"Eliza," he breathed, "you look better than I feared. Worse than I'd hoped. The relics are all safe at the Museum, thanks to you both."

She managed a faint smile in response.

"You're the one who sent them into this?" Simon insisted, stepping forward.

"No, I'm the one who asked for the Veil to be recovered. Your daughters decided how to answer that call," Solan answered evenly, "and they did so with courage and clarity."

Beatrice's lips formed a tight line, but she nodded. "Even without the Order watching over them properly."

Solan approached the window with his hands clasped behind his back. "I didn't come here to argue. I came here to say thank you. And to offer a way forward." He turned toward Eliza and Esme. "You've both seen what lies beneath the Order's public face, the parts we usually don't share with new initiates — the ghosts. The betrayals. The cost."

Eliza's gaze narrowed and her thumbs flew across the smartphone keyboard and she held the screen up for him to read. *You're saying we can't go back to our lives. I just want to go home to my cat.*

Solan nodded. "Eugenia will miss him, but we'll bring him home once you're released. Your life won't be the way it was before. No more gift shops, no more lab-only jobs. You've crossed into the field now. That journey doesn't end with one relic."

Esme stood, her eyes uncertain. "So what happens?"

"Once Eliza's recovered, you'll both begin formal field training. Not punishment — *preparation*. What you accomplished without it was extraordinary, if ... let's just say *enthusiastically reckless*."

The corners of his mouth flickered with something like amusement. He reached into his coat pocket and produced two small scrolls bound with deep blue ribbons sealed in wax — the formal seals of Order assignment.

Esme looked at the scrolls, then up at Solan. "What if we say no?"

"Then you walk away. No oaths, no assignments, no chains. But understand —" his voice softened, "the Veil and the Brooch know you. You've touched a Divine plane. Power like that doesn't go away just because you ignore it."

Beatrice looked up at him, her eyes hardening in an expression she'd clearly passed down to her eldest daughter. "Solan, what are you turning them into?"

He met her gaze, his response resolute.

"What the world needs."

Craving more? Eliza and Esme's journey is far from over.

Continue the adventure in Book 2 of the *Manifest Destiny Series: The Night Doctor's Blade.*

Turn the page to find out where fate leads the Wrens next!

EXCERPT: THE NIGHT DOCTOR'S BLADE

BOOK 2 OF THE MANIFEST DESTINY SERIES

Present Day, Somewhere in the Scottish Highlands
The road to Glen Craeg was little more than a memory etched into the moor — an uneven trail of moss-covered stones swallowed by gorse and peat. The sisters left the car miles behind, trading headlights for torches and the soft crunch of boots against the frostbitten heather.

A low mist clung to the hills, curling around their legs like a living thing. In the distance, the silhouette of the glen yawned wide, cradled by crags like sleeping giants. The ruins of the old witch's croft leaned into the wind near the loch's edge, its crumbling stones slick with time and covered in ivy as thick as secrets.

Somewhere in the distance, a lone curlew cried — long and mournful, as if echoing a memory. Esme paused, tilting her head.

"You hear that?"

Eliza stilled. It wasn't a bird call. It was a lullaby. Faint. Half-caught in the fog. A tune not sung by any living voice.

Around them, the mist thickened, not with malice but memory. This was sacred ground — where the veil between two worlds thinned. Here, the past wasn't gone. The air crackled with old magic, the kind that never truly dies.

Esme ran her fingers along the edge of the weathered stone wall, etched with ancient runes. Scribbles in some ancient medium — charcoal perhaps — harkened images of dragons and monsters. It told not just of legends, though. It was a sign. A ward. A warning. Or maybe a promise.

Beneath the ruins, the old root cellar waited — a circle of stones sunken into the earth, overgrown and half-buried. The entrance was marked by a cairn shaped like a sleeping serpent. The last known resting place of Morag, the Widow of the Glen.

This was where the missing artifact – the Last Dragon's Egg – might be kept, if anywhere still held its warmth. But they'd need to earn the old widow's trust. Glen Craeg did not give up its ghosts — or its dragons — easily.

The sisters stood before the serpent cairn, their torches scanning the moss-slick stones for signs of a hidden door or secret niche. Esme crouched beside a tuft of something growing in the dark recesses of the root cellar. Beneath it, carved into the foundation, was a mosaic of obsidian scales set in a spiral pattern — some missing, others dulled with age. At its center, a shallow bowl etched with ancient runes and a faintly glowing symbol that resembled a dragon's eye.

Eliza knelt beside it, wincing as pain tugged the muscles in her neck. She couldn't speak, not properly, not since Maelis' blade had silenced her. Instead, she traced the edge of the bowl with two fingers, brows furrowed. Her breath steamed in the morning air, but her focus remained unshaken.

Esme watched her carefully. "It's a song puzzle," she murmured. "A lullaby — Morag's lullaby." Eliza glanced up, nodding, a smile brightening her typically stoic face. "Maybe the only way to awaken the widow is to sing her song?"

Eliza nodded slowly. She pointed to Esme, then to the bowl. *You have to sing.* Eliza's eyes spoke the words her voice could not.

Esme swallowed hard. "Me? I don't know the song."

Eliza tapped her temple, then placed her hand on Esme's chest. She closed her eyes and drew in a breath. *You do. You can feel it.* Forcing it, Eliza managed a faint hum in a tune Esme almost remembered like a ghost from her childhood. Then it came to her, the crackling voice of their grandmother.

The tune was one not just every Scot knew, but one almost everyone on the planet knew. It was a song that united nations and spoke of happier times — sung every year, like clockwork, to harken in the new year. But Esme remembered the version their grandmother sang.

She paused to clear her throat, aware of what Eliza's throat must feel like as nerves gripped her like a hand tightening around her neck. She took a deep breath and let her voice be guided by her memories of her grandmother.

Hush now, my wee one, close yer eyes
The stars are climbin' high—
The heather dreams beneath the moon,
And so, my love shall I.

The tentative timbre of her song faded, as the beauty of her voice reverberated off the stones. The acoustics of the chamber put the Aldwych Theatre to shame. It gave Esme courage to continue.

Lie still, my flame, the night is kind,
The mist guards every glen—
And should ye wake, I'll sing again,
'Til day returns, amen.
No hunter's horn shall stir ye sleep,
No storm nor shadows grim—

For while I breathe, ye're safe wi' me,

In earth, in sky, in hymn.

The glow of the dragon eye in the stone strengthened, throbbing with a heartbeat that matched the tempo. Eliza encouraged Esme to continue, like a conductor's baton guided her hand. Eliza tried to sing along, but her voice wouldn't cooperate, and it sounded more like a croaking toad than a song. It didn't stop her from trying, if only in whispers.

So dreams of flight 'bove loch and brae,

O' winds that rise and turn—

And shall I keep yer ember bright,

'Til fire and soul return.

Those were the words Esme intended to sing, but those were not the words that came from her mouth. Instead, the speech was distorted, and the words slurred into something more, dragon-like.

Zar drāvak ir'syl thurin'kaar,

Vel'kyn drōmah zhelen.

Aruv zharneth kal-drien far,

Tal shur vakaar en'en.

The runes carved into the walls—even those worn by time—flickered to life, casting a puce glow in the dark cellar. The mosaic began to turn, clicking softly as the pieces shifted into different places. A low rumble echoed beneath their feet.

Suddenly, the mist above the cairn coalesced, gathering and twisting until it formed the ghostly image of a woman. Majestic. Ancient.

Eliza looked up, her breath catching. The vision of Morag gained her physical form. She was slight, but sound — her eyes bright but cautious. Her long white locks were knotted and twisted into braids and cords, charms tied into the tresses. She wore a dark gown from a long forgotten time with a swatch of plaid pinned over her shoulder. The Widow inspect-ed the girls, then bowed not to Esme, but to Eliza.

Behind the witch, where the dim light only caught her silhouette, stretched the impossible shadow of something else entirely – a great ser-pent, crowned and coiling, its massive body breaching the shimmering light like the Monster, breaking the surface of the nearby loch. It was not a shadow, nor a trick of the mist. It was her truth made visible.

The witch's voice echoed across the glen — not with sound, but with memory. A single word settled into their minds:

"Prove."

Then the cairn slid open with a hiss of displaced air, revealing a chamber lit with bioluminescent moss which grew on the walls, and up a single pedestal. Upon it rested an egg the size of a pumpkin, shimmering with iridescent scales, and pulsing with life.

Before they could take it, Morag stepped into their path, her voice deeper now.

"Only one may carry it. The one who remembers fire."

Eliza closed her eyes. She could still feel the burn of the ritual, the seer of the blade, and the moment death kissed her and left her changed.

Esme reached for the egg—then paused. "It's you, isn't it?" she whis-pered. "She means *you.*"

Eliza nodded, trembling. Her fingers hovered just above the shell, warmth radiating from it. She remembered fire. And now, so did the egg.

Eliza's throat grew tighter with every breath. Her hand contacted the shell, but rather than burn, it warmed her to the core, the chill of an October night forgotten. It hummed, and Eliza was aware of the pulsing heartbeat within.

A deep, seismic thrum echoed through the chamber. The ground heaved beneath them. Rocks tumbled from the reinforced walls. Eliza caught the egg as the pedestal beneath it folded open like a blooming flower. The chamber shifted. Stone ground against stone. The runes flickered on the walls, racing, not in warning, but in judgment.

Esme stumbled back as the mist coalesced again, this time forming a draconic figure, spectral and ancient. It was not hostile—but it was watching. This echo of a dragon appeared nothing like the CGI-generated *Smaug* portrayed in *The Lord of the Rings* movies. This dragon was more delicate, more Celtic. He loomed above them as the ceiling of the chamber seemed to rise, or perhaps the floor lowered. His eyes were soft, filled with recognition.

Eliza clutched the egg to her chest just as the floor fell out from beneath them. A hidden pit yawned wide—but instead of plummeting, they were caught, midair, suspected by a column of golden swirling light.

The runes spiraled around her like living ink, crawling across her skin. The egg pulsed against her heart. The wound inside her throat began to burn. Not with pain, but with heat, as though the fire of the dragon was being poured into her.

The voices of the spectral witch and dragons spoke as one:

"One must be forged anew to carry fire. Flesh must remember death. But the soul must choose to live."

Flames erupted around the edge of the pit — it burned, but Eliza was not consumed. The flames moved to form a circle. Esme rushed forward, but the flames pushed her back. She wanted to aid her sister, who was still fragile from her recent death. She wanted to bear the burden of carrying the egg. Eliza had been through enough already.

Like Frodo bearing the ring to Mordor, Eliza hadn't been the same since leaving the Nest nearly a year ago. Like Samwise, Esme would have borne each of her sister's struggles — if only for a little while — if she could. But this was Eliza's trial alone.

Esme felt the weight of her own burden come over her in that moment. The shadow of the vision world into which she often crossed came over her, and she could see the Widow of the Glen—Morag—place the egg deep into the earth, away from the eyes of men who lusted for the power it might offer. She saw the memory of the young dragon as he nuzzled her cheek with his horn, distraught that its clutch-mate had not hatched. Then she saw the moment of her sister's death, Maelis's blade. Clarity came when she focused on the silver blade and realized it was shaped like the dragon's horn. She saw the haze of blood. Gushing. Spurting. Spraying.

Then there was something else — a burst of light, and a heartbeat not her own.

The chamber rumbled again, and the egg cracked, ever so slightly. The hairline fracture allowed the light within to illuminate the darkness.

A piercing screech like a newborn baby's cry echoed around them, and Esme came out of the world of shadows to see her sister cradling the new life in her arms. The dragonling gazed into Eliza's eye with a look of wonder, its first moments in the world as traumatic as Eliza's last.

Esme took a tentative step toward the creature that looked so sweet and innocent. It hiccupped. A puff of smoke billowed from its nostrils. Esme stepped back, matching gazes with Eliza.

"How come you get to be the Mother of Dragons?"

"Ladies!" a voice found them. Eliza gazed up and saw Solan Virell, the Grand Aegis of the Order, squatting down over the collapsed cairn. "Well done. Normally, we would begin Esme's trial right away, but we don't have the luxury."

"My trial?" Esme moved closer to her sister, but the dragon nipped at her, and she recoiled, hopping away from danger. "I thought this was *our* trial."

"Each acolyte faces their own tests, Esme." He said, coming down the steps that neither of the girls had noticed. "But yours will have to wait. We just received word that one of our Agents was attacked in Romania. We need teams to provide support, and the High Council agrees you are the right ones for the job. Eugenia said she'd be happy to watch Faraday for a few more weeks."

Solan paused, turning to the Widow who stood with an expression that suggested she was put off by his sudden arrival. "Sorry to cut the show short, love." He addressed her with a familiarity of old friends. "The girls are needed elsewhere. Are you satisfied?"

"Auch aye," the woman said, picking up the broken egg, closing it. The dragon in Eliza's arms disappeared, startling her.

"Wait. What?" Esme gasped. Eliza didn't look any less confused.

Morag moved closer to Solan, running her hand along his cheek. "Dinnae ferget tae bring the haggis fer Burn's Night. Will I see ye then?"

"Yes, of course," Solan leaned in and kissed her cheek.

"Thank you for your help, again." he said, turning back to the girls. "As I was saying ..."

The vision of the hidden cairn faded into nothingness, and with it, the Widow of the Glen and her egg were gone.

Eliza put a hand in the middle of Solan's chest, lifting her hand into an arc, questions filling her eyes.

"Oh, well," he said, "we have a formal alliance with certain individuals to aid in testing our new acolytes. Morag, well, she's a fine auld girl." His Scottish accent wasn't entirely convincing. "There are those with true magic, and we're lucky she works for us."

Eliza shook her head, and turned away, clearly done with the whole affair.

"When do we leave?" Esme asked.

"The Secretary is making arrangements for a flight this evening," he said. "You have a few hours to get something to eat, sleep, shower, whatever you need."

Eliza tapped her wrist as if she wore a watch, then lifted her hands in question.

"I know it's not much time," Solan said, "but if the Healer's Shard of Arkanos falls into the hands of the Covenant, it won't be just a plague on mankind — it'll be the slaughter of millions. Contagion run amok. By the time anyone sees what is happening, the rot will have set in, and no doctor in the world can cut it out."